BROTHERS

I WILL FIND OUT WHO DID THIS AND I WILL MAKE THEM PAY

IN ARMS

PENNY DEE

Brothers in Arms
Kings of Mayhem MC Series Book 2

Penny Dee

Disclaimer: The material in this book contains graphic language and sexual content and is intended for mature audiences, ages 18 and older.

ISBN: 978-1795662697

Editing by Elaine at Allusion Graphics
Proofreading by Stephanie Burdett
Formatting by Swish Design & Editing
Cover design by Marisa at Cover Me Darling
Cover image Copyright 2019

DEDICATION

To Bam Bam.

PATH OF FAMILY

The Calley Family
Hutch Calley (deceased) married Sybil Stone
Griffin Calley
Garrett Calley (deceased)

Griffin Calley married Peggy Russell
Isaac Calley
Abby Calley

Garrett Calley married Veronica Western
Chance Calley
Cade Calley
Caleb Calley
Chastity Calley

The Parrish Family
Jude Parrish married Connie Walker
Jackson Parrish
Samuel Parrish (deceased)

Jackie Parrish married Lady Winter
Bolt Parrish
Indigo Parrish

The Western Family
Michael 'Bull' Western
Veronica 'Ronnie' Western

ORIGINAL CHAPTER

Kings of Mayhem MC

Bull (President)
Jackie (VP)
Cade
Caleb
Isaac
Grunt (SIA)
Davey
Tex
Vader
Joker
Cool Hand
Elias
Griffin
Jacob
Matlock
Maverick
Tully
Irish

Nitro

Hawke

Freebird

Ari

Picasso

Caveman

Chance (on tour)

Reuben (honorary member)

Employees of the Kings

Red (Chef, clubhouse housekeeper)

Mrs Stephens (Bookkeeper, administration)

BROTHERS

I WILL FIND OUT WHO DID THIS AND I WILL MAKE THEM PAY

IN ARMS

PENNY DEE

PROLOGUE

CADE

Kneeling in your loved one's blood and having them die in your arms changes you.

I know it changed me.

When Isaac died, my heart hardened.

My anger was palpable.

As I watched them remove his lifeless body from the pool of his blood, I vowed revenge. Fury thundered through my veins. Life changed in a heartbeat, and every part of my being could feel it. Rage tore through me, spiraling into every nerve and fiber, every muscle, every tendon, every shard of my shattered heart. Pain ripped at my guts and opened me up. But it was nothing, *nothing*, like my need for retribution.

Bull and Caleb showed up. God knows who called them.

Despite Indy's protests, I sent her home in the safety of a police cruiser while I followed Buckman and the ambulance to the county morgue. I didn't know why, but I needed answers, and for some reason, I felt they were with Isaac's body.

Isaac's body.

My chest caved in under the weight of my grief.

"You can't be here," Buckman said as I bounded the steps of the county morgue.

"Try stopping me."

He pressed a hand into my chest to stop me from going inside. His old brown eyes sought out mine. "Don't make me arrest you, son."

I expelled a deep breath of air. "Isaac is in there…"

"I know." Buckman stepped in front of the doorway. "And you need to let us do our job, Cade. Let Zachariah take care of him."

Zachariah Sumstad was the county medical examiner.

I sucked in a deep breath and looked away. My grief was dizzying. My head spun. I wanted to rip someone's head off to somehow release the growing agony inside of me. I wanted to find out who did this to Isaac and choke the hell out of them and watch the life drain from their eyes.

I inhaled deeply, the muscles in my jaw clenching. "You find out who did this. And you let me know." My voice was low, dangerous, and dripping with a barely controlled rage.

Buckman nodded. "As is protocol."

I leaned in. "No. I want this guy."

"I can't do that, Cade."

"Then I'll just make sure it happens. You won't be able to protect him."

Buckman put a hand on my shoulder. "One step at a time, son."

I turned and stormed down the steps to my bike. Then, gunning the engine, roared off into the morning.

I was going to find out who killed Isaac.

CHAPTER 1

CADE

You can see the moment when someone realizes their life is never going to be the same. It's almost as if you can see the cogs working behind their eyes as they try to make sense of what they've just heard. What does this mean for me? How will life be from this moment on? When I pulled up to Cherry and Isaac's little house just out of town, Buckman was already knocking on her door.

I roared up the driveway and came to a quick halt.

Cherry answered the door and took one look at Buckman, with his hat against his chest, as he said the words that would change her life forever.

Isaac was dead.

I ran across the lawn toward her. I saw her frown. Saw her shake her head as if to say, no, you're wrong. Saw her knees go weak and the dazed look on her face as she fell against the door.

I climbed the porch steps two at a time, brushed past Buckman and wrapped my arms around her.

"It's not true," she said desperately. "Tell him, Cade. Tell him he's wrong."

I held her tightly against my chest. "I'm so sorry, Cherry."

She pushed me away. "Not you, too. Why are you both saying this? He's alive."

She fled to the kitchen and picked up her cell phone from the countertop, her fingers shaking as she dialed Isaac's number.

"He was picking up pie for me," she said desperately, ending the call when nobody answered, then quickly redialing. Somewhere in the blurry depths of my mind I could see Isaac's phone ringing unanswered in the county morgue, covered in his blood. "He's coming home to fix the water pump. I'm making him chili for dinner." Her whole body trembled and tears flowed down her cheeks as her thoughts frantically bounced all over the place. Her body already knew he was gone but there was still a tiny shred in her mind that refused to believe it. "He likes the way I make his chili. I use the peppers from the garden."

I crossed the room and gently took the phone from her, then pulled her into my arms again. There was no need for words. Her mind let go of the last scrap of hope and the terrible acceptance sank in. She weakened against me and slowly collapsed to the floor.

"Her sister Ashlee lives three doors down," I said to Buckman. "You better go get her."

When Buckman left, I guided Cherry to her feet and led her over to the couch.

"What happened?" She sobbed, reaching up to play with the crown pendant around her neck. Her hands were shaking.

"He was shot."

"Shot?" She looked at me in disbelief. "By who?"

"I don't know."

She stood up. "Who would want to shoot Isaac? It doesn't make any sense. Why would anyone want him dead?"

"I will find out," I said. My chest filled with pain when I thought about him lying on the road, coughing up mouthfuls of dark blood. And then that horrifying moment when the second bullet hit him between the eyes. I could still hear it echoing throughout the valley. "And when I do, I am going to make them pay."

"Mommy?" Came the little voice behind us. We both looked around to see Braxton standing in the doorway, rubbing his eyes and looking confused. He was in his Spiderman pajamas and looked so little. So vulnerable. A silent growl rolled through me. Braxton would grow up without his father. He would never get to share the bond of father and son, or share the milestones of his life. He would never learn from the man who'd loved him so fiercely. Who had cried when he was born and had proudly inked himself with his son's name within hours of his birth. Isaac was always a tough guy. Big and brawn. But when it came to his son, he was as soft as butter.

"Oh, baby," Cherry went to him and scooped him up. She held him close to her, unable to hold her tears back.

"What's wrong, Mommy? Why are you crying?"

My throat closed with a cold ache as rage and heartache fused in every cell of my body. Cherry sat down with her son on her lap and I watched her struggle with her words. My fingers itched with anger at my sides and I had to curl them into a fist to stop. I would find who did this and I was going to make them bleed until their heart stopped beating.

"It's Daddy. . ." Cherry stammered. Tears spilled down her cheeks and her chin quivered.

Braxton started to cry. "What's wrong with Daddy? Why are you crying?"

Cherry summoned her inner strength. "Do you remember when Fetch got sick and we had to take him to the doggy doctor?"

Braxton nodded and his big blue eyes brimmed with more tears.

"And remember how we couldn't bring him home because God needed him back in heaven?"

Again, Braxton nodded, but this time his lip curled and his chin quivered.

"Well, baby, God needed Daddy back. And this morning—" Her pain cut her off, and she inhaled deeply to calm herself, and then slowly exhaled. She knew the next few words out of her mouth would be something her son would always remember. She knew her husband's death was going to leave a lasting scar on her little boy's heart, and I could see her wrestle with finding the right words. "This morning, God came and took Daddy back because He needed him up in heaven."

Braxton's eyes widened. "You mean Daddy's gone?"

Cherry struggled to keep her composure as she nodded. And I watched in silent agony as little Braxton's face crumpled and his tears fell down his chubby cheeks.

"But I don't want Daddy to go to heaven," he cried. "I don't want Daddy to be gone. I want him here with me."

"I know, Mommy doesn't want him to be gone either, but, baby, we don't get a choice."

Braxton's grief turned to sudden anger. He frowned and thrust his hands down. "No! I don't want him to go." He wriggled off Cherry's lap and threw himself onto the ground and pounded his fist into the carpet. "I don't want him to go. I don't want him to go."

I knelt down so I was eye level with him. But it was a struggle to get my first words out. "Hey, little man, I know you don't like this. None of us do. But, buddy, you need to be strong for your mom, okay? You're the man of the house now. Mommy is going to need your help. Especially when your little brother or sister comes along."

The mention of his sibling eased some of the anger from his sad face. His tear-drenched eyes lit up for a moment.

"I will help her. I will." He straightened. "I'm the big brother."

I smiled, but it was hard as fuck to get my face muscles to work.

"That's my boy." I ruffled his hair and fist bumped him. "You gotta stay strong for your mama."

He stood up onto his little feet and went to his mom, climbing up and throwing his arms around her neck.

Cherry held him to her as another sob wracked her body. "It's going to be okay, baby."

"I will help you, Mommy. I will. I promise."

The front door opened and Ashlee ran in. Still dressed in her pajamas and robe, she went straight to her sister and nephew, and threw her arms around them, holding them tight as she sobbed.

Buckman hung back in the doorway.

"Cherry's family is on their way down from Tennessee," he said. He played with his hat in his hands. "Son, I'm going to need you to come down to the station to give a statement."

I nodded. "I'll meet you down there."

After he left, I sat with Cherry and Ashlee, but I needed to get out of there. The grief was closing in on me and I felt a restlessness to do something. When I was sure Cherry was calm, I said goodbye, and feeling hollow, walked into the early morning sunlight and climbed on my bike.

Isaac was dead.

But it wasn't because God needed him back.

He was dead because someone had murdered him.

And I was going to find out who it was and send them to their grave.

CHAPTER 2

INDY

I had the police deputy drop me at my mom's. She was waiting on the little porch out front, and as soon as I climbed the steps, we threw our arms around one another. As we parted, she put her hands on either side of my face. "Are you okay?"

I nodded but my chin trembled and my eyes welled with tears.

"It happened so fast . . ." My words trailed off, caught in my tight throat.

"And Cade? Is he okay?" I remembered the look of agony on Cade's face as they loaded Isaac's body into the ambulance. I shook my head. "He's devastated."

"Bull rang Ronnie and told her what happened."

A lot of phones would ring this morning with the news. By now, the entire club and their families would know.

"Abby . . ." I whispered, suddenly aware she would have heard. Alarmed, I looked at my mom. "I have to go to her."

"I can drive you," she said.

I raced, frantically listing the things in my head that I needed in order to get out the door. Keys. Handbag. Phone.

Dammit, where was my phone?

"Indy," my mom said calmly.

But I ignored her. I had to find my phone. I checked in the kitchen, the dining room, the—

"Indy!" My mom's voice stopped me. I looked across at her, frantic because I couldn't find my phone and I had to get to Abby's quickly.

"What?"

She gestured to my clothes. "Don't you think you should change your clothes first?"

I looked down at my shirt. It was covered in blood spatter.

Isaac's blood.

I stared at it, my hands shaking as I pulled at the stained fabric and held it out in front of me. That's when I noticed the dried blood on my hands and up my arms.

Isaac's blood.

The realization seeped into me.

My face crumpled.

Isaac was dead.

I fled to the bathroom and thrust my hands under the running faucet, furiously scrubbing at my fingers and wrists. Bloody water filled the basin and swirled down the drain in a rust-colored whirlpool. I grabbed more soap and lathered it onto my skin, washing it until the water ran clear. I turned off the faucet and began drying my hands but stopped when I caught a glance of my reflection in the mirror. I straightened and stared numbly. Isaac's blood was speckled across my face like bright red freckles.

I felt Mom's hand on my shoulder.

"You need to catch a breath, baby girl," she said gently. She turned me around and handed me a towel. "Have a shower. Collect yourself. And then you'll be ready to help Abby."

Mom was right. I needed to compose myself before I saw her. Abby needed me to be strong. Calm. Collected. *Everything that I wasn't right now.*

Suddenly overcome with love and gratefulness for my mom, I threw my arms around her and hugged her tightly to me, absorbing the comfort of her soothing mom-rubs up and down my back.

"You're okay," she said reassuringly to me as we parted.

I exhaled deeply and nodded, every ounce of me heavy with the numbness of Isaac's murder.

When mom left, I closed the door and stripped off. Stepping into the shower, I let the warm water wash Isaac's blood from my skin. I washed my hair and scrubbed at my skin with the shower loofah I found hanging from the tap, and scrubbed under my nails. Once clean, I dried off and put on some clean clothes, feeling grateful that my clothes were still here and not at the new house. *The new house.* We were due to move in this weekend.

I sat on the edge of the bath and drew in a deep breath in some attempt to calm the chaos.

And then I started to cry.

Hard.

My hands shook and my chest caved with the weight of my grief as the events of the past couple of hours caught up with me. Isaac was dead. And he had died right in front of me.

I dropped my head to my hands and sobbed, trying desperately to force the images of his last moments out of my mind.

His struggle for breath.

His fight for life.

His fear.

The way his blood soaked hand had reached for me, tugging at my shirt, begging me to help him.

The whip of the bullet as it punched into his forehead.

I sank to the floor and buried my face in my arm, my body wracked with pain.

I had loved him.

My whole life.

And now my friend was gone.

I sobbed harder and let my grief take over until I couldn't cry anymore. Until my self-preservation finally showed up and I was able to steady my nerves and calm my heart.

I drew in a deep breath and wiped the tears from my eyes. And when I was sure I was able to hold it together, I rose to my feet and went to the basin and splashed water on my tear-stained face.

I had to hold it together for Abby.

And Cade.

This was going to devastate him.

Dressed, I felt calmer. Steadier. Composed. Strong enough to see Abby. I went downstairs and my mom was waiting for me in the kitchen.

"You look better," she said. She came and stood in front of me, taking me by the arms. "You've got this, okay."

Mom drove us to Abby's. It took us twenty minutes and I barely waited for the car to stop before running up Abby's driveway to her front door. I didn't even knock, I burst through it. Abby was at the dining table, an untouched cup of coffee in front of her. When she saw me her face crumpled and she started to cry, her whole body shaking with her grief. I went to her and wrapped my arms around her, letting her cry uncontrollably into my shoulder. And even though I didn't want to, I started to cry with her.

"You were with him?" she asked, pulling back, her icy blue eyes red from crying.

I nodded. "We were coming back from Head Quarters. Someone set fire to it. We went out there to check it out. On the way back . . ." I had to pause to catch my breath as memories floated up and made my heart hurt. ". . . it happened so fast."

Abby started to cry again.

"I want to see him," she sobbed.

Ronnie and Mom exchanged concerned looks.

"That's not a good idea," I said gently.

"I don't care, I want to see him."

I thought of the bullet in Isaac's forehead.

"Honey, he won't look like him," I said, my voice shaky. "He was shot in the head."

Abby's face collapsed in agony. She struggled to breathe and exhaled slowly, trying to regain her composure, but failed when she thought about what I was telling her. She ran her shaking hands up and down her thighs to try and steady them.

"He's gone, Abby. And seeing him that way . . . it's only going to upset you more."

"I don't care," she said through gritted teeth.

"Are you sure that's a good idea, baby?" Ronnie asked.

Abby stood up so fast her chair almost toppled over.

"We grew in a womb together for thirty-seven weeks. We came into this world together. For thirty years he has been my best friend. Not just my twin. We talk every single day and tell each other everything." Her face collapsed again as another spear of pain ran through her heart, because in that moment she realized she would never hear her brother's voice again. She turned to look at me. "Will you take me?"

I thought about it, and then nodded. I knew how it felt to lose a brother. I knew what the big hole in her heart felt like and I understood the importance of what she wanted to do. She would never share another moment with him, unless she did this.

"Good," she said with a newfound calm. "I'm going to get my jacket and then I'm going to go see my brother."

CHAPTER 3

CADE

The frigid air of the morgue made the hair on the back of my neck stand up. It was like the subtle stench of death lingered in every breath you took, reminding you that the cold kept the reek at bay, and that out there in the heat the smell would be much worse.

I was waiting for Indy and Abby inside when they arrived. Indy saw me and quickly came to me, wrapping her arms around my waist and pressing her face to my chest. The familiar warmth of her embrace and the scent of her was a welcome break from the tortuous pain in my heart. Her scent. Her touch. It brought me the only relief I'd felt since this morning and I closed my eyes, pressing my lips to her hair and savoring the comfort even though I knew it was going to be brief.

"What are you doing here?" she whispered.

"Mom rang . . . are you crazy? Bringing Abby here?" I whispered back.

"I'm right here you know," Abby said.

She came to me and fell into my arms.

"I'm sorry, Abs," I breathed, holding her tight.

"Don't be angry at Indy. I was coming here with or without her." She looked up at me. "I need to say goodbye."

I nodded. She was an adult. She knew what she needed to do and I wasn't going to try to stop her.

Camila, the morgue assistant, greeted us and then led us out the back where the bodies were kept prior to being moved to the funeral home.

"Isaac's hasn't been autopsied," she explained. "Dr. Sumstad will be doing that tomorrow. In the meanwhile, we've taken good care of him."

Pain rose up from my core and I drew in a deep breath as we followed her into the cool room. As we waited for her to show us Isaac, Indy's fingers curled into mine.

"Ready?" Camila asked. When we nodded, she opened the stainless steel drawer and pulled back the sheet covering Isaac's body.

A strangled gasp came from Abby, and a pain as vicious as anything I had ever known tightened my chest.

Isaac was the pale color of death. He had been washed clean of all the blood and brain matter, and his hair hung in cold, damp tendrils off his face, concealing the crater in the back of his head where the bullet had exited. His eyes were only half-closed, and I was knocked on my ass by the milky lifelessness of them as they stared back at us, unseeing and empty. His mouth was closed, his lips pale, and just above his nose, right between his eyes, was the blackened, star-shaped bullet hole.

"No," Abby sobbed.

Her knees went weak and I pulled her to me to stop her from collapsing. But I had no words to comfort her. My throat was cold and tight, strangled by grief. I felt her falter in my arms, her body wracked with pain as she sobbed into my chest.

"No," she cried again, shaking her head.

She pulled away from me, and I watched with a stony face as she stepped closer to her brother and took his cold hand in hers. Her chin quivered as she tried to sniff back her tears. At first she just opened her mouth, but no words came out.

She exhaled deeply, tears spilling from her eyes with every blink.

"I just wanted you to know that I wouldn't have wanted anyone else as my twin, Isaac. You were the best big brother that a girl could have hoped for. Even if you were only ninety-seconds older." Her face screwed up as a rush of pain overcame her, but she drew in a deep breath to steady herself and licked her lips to steady her quaking chin. "It's okay. We'll be okay. So you go in peace, you hear me? And when it's time, we'll see each other again."

I could barely contain my tears. They stabbed at my eyes and my face was stiff with the pain of holding them in. I looked at Indy and she was crying, tears streaming down her cheeks as she watched Abby say goodbye to her twin brother.

I couldn't look anymore. I had to get out of there.

I needed to breathe.

# CHAPTER 4

CADE

It rained the day we buried Isaac. Thunder rumbled in a stormy sky. We rode in the usual procession of motorcycles through the streets of Destiny, the lights of our bikes cutting through the gloom of a cold fall day. I rode behind Bull, my heart heavy with pain and my face so stiff with grief I didn't even feel the first drops of rain when they began to fall. I just rode.

When we arrived at the church, Indy waited for me at the base of the stairs. She had ridden with Lady, my sister Chastity, and my mom. She took my hand in hers and I barely held it together when I looked across the parking lot and saw Cherry and little Braxton making their way toward us. Oh Christ. Braxton's face was crumpled with sadness and he looked so lost and confused, it tore me up inside.

I let go of Indy's hand and went to them, scooping Braxton up and hugging him tight. Cherry started to sob against my mom's shoulder, which set Braxton off.

"Hey," I croaked. "It's okay, buddy. I got you."

I tried to hand him back to Cherry, but the little dude wouldn't let go. He wound his arms tighter around my neck and buried his face into my shoulder. Cherry looked pleadingly at me. She wanted me to hold onto him, so I nodded and took him with me. I would be strong for him. For Isaac. For me. But when I walked through the doorway and I saw Isaac's coffin at the end of the aisle, I faltered, and for the first time in my life, my knees were weak. Pain crashed through me, colliding with a grief so violent I was momentarily unable to move. It took Braxton burying his face into my neck to get me moving. Somehow I found my seat in the pew. Somehow I got through the service without breaking apart. I just focused on the coffin and let my anger take reign.

Vengeance. I'd be lying if the word hadn't frequented the establishment of my brain a lot in the past few days. But this time it appeared like an epiphany. Blood red and backed by the most destructive emotion of all: rage. I would find out who did this to my cousin and I would take from them what they had taken from Isaac.

I stared straight ahead. My head full of memories. My heart full of pain. My entire body consumed by an overwhelming need for revenge. And somewhere in that church, during the service for my slayed cousin, my grief turned into a seething and unrelenting obsession for vengeance.

Dire Straits "*Brothers In Arms*" played as I helped Maverick, Caleb, Bull, Vader, and Abby carry Isaac's coffin out to the awaiting hearse. Wind whipped around our legs and my heart goddamn broke as they lowered my cousin into the ground. It was too much to bear. Filled with agony, I walked away, unable to watch Isaac's cut disappear into the ground with his coffin. I climbed on my bike and gunned the engine, riding off into the storm.

CHAPTER 5

INDY

Cade had changed. He'd turned cold with hate. Despondent with grief. Quietly simmering with rage.

I hoped it would get better in time. But I'd seen the look on his face today at the funeral. I'd seen the cold, hard darkness in his eyes and the tightened tick of muscles as he clenched his jaw. He was consumed with rage. Overtaken by grief. Mad with whatever darkness was taking control of him.

When he'd walked away, I had let him go. I'd gone to the wake at the clubhouse and spent the next four hours keeping myself occupied by serving food and cleaning up paper plates and cups. I was cleaning up outside on the patio when Isaac's mom, Peggy, cornered me. She was smoking and taking angry sips of wine from a plastic cup, followed by angry puffs on her cigarette. I hadn't seen her in twenty years. She had walked out on Griffin not long after he went into a wheelchair.

"Well, well, well, if it isn't little Indigo Parrish. Haven't you grown up to be somethin'," she said, her over-made-up eyes rolling over me with something close to resentment.

"Peggy," I replied with a nod. I had never liked Isaac's mom. She was loud and brazen, and she had a sharp tongue.

"I heard you left town," she said, her tone accusatory and challenging.

When I thought about Peggy Calley, I automatically recalled the memory of her and Garrett Calley having sex on the washing machine while her husband, Ronnie, and other club members were outside having a barbeque. I had come inside for a drink of water. Hearing a giggle and some muffled voices down the hallway, my eight-year-old curiosity had gotten the better of me and I had snuck down the hallway and peeked through the slatted laundry door. Peggy had been sitting on the washing machine and Garrett Calley was standing between her parted legs, his jeans around his ankles as he fucked her.

"I came back for my father's funeral," I replied, reminding myself that this was her son's funeral and I should probably be a little more tolerant of her than she deserved.

"And you stayed?"

I busied myself with picking up trash left on the barbeque table and putting it into the garbage bag in my hand. "Looks that way."

I heard her scoff and looked up. Peggy Calley would be in her early fifties, but she looked like a woman in her sixties. The biker life and whatever cesspit she had fallen into after abandoning her family had taken its toll on her.

But she had just lost her son, and my heart felt for her. We all had each other. The club. Me and Cade. While she had nothing and no-one.

"I'm sorry about Isaac," I said, that familiar sting of pain twisting in my chest.

Cold eyes paused on me. "Yeah, well, can't say I'm surprised. You live by the sword, you die by the sword. Isn't that what they say?" She drew heavily on her cigarette and blew the smoke toward me. "I always told him that nothing good would come of him joining this stupid fucking club. Told him to stay clear of the lifestyle. I said, 'Isaac, look at what that club did to your daddy. Look at what it did to your Uncle Garrett. Ain't nothing good is going to come from you becoming a King.'" She scoffed and drew on her cigarette again. "Of course, he didn't listen to me. Damn fool. Just like his goddamn father."

Peggy had walked out on her family when Isaac and Abby were nine years old. She disappeared for years. No one knew where she was or what she was doing, or whom she was with. Birthdays came and went with no word from her. No card. No phone call. No letter. Milestones were missed. Isaac could be forgiven for not listening to his mother when she finally turned up all those years later.

"I heard you had left town. Broke up with Cade after he cheated on you. Took off and became a fancy doctor," she said. "I thought, good for her. She got out. She got away. She broke a Calley heart." Her eyes flashed with pathetic delight at the idea. Then, they narrowed and she took a step toward me, shaking her head with judgmental disbelief. "Yet here the fuck you are, a fancy-assed doctor picking up trash at a biker funeral."

I dropped the garbage bag at her feet and straightened. "Have you got something you want to say to me, Peggy?"

She scoffed and sucked on her cigarette again.

"Just that it is a real shame. A beauty like you, getting sucked in by a Calley. He's cheated on you once before, Indy. Mark my words, that boy will cheat on you again."

"That was a long time ago when we were just kids. Cade isn't like that."

She sneered. "Don't kid yourself, young lady. They're all like that. Every single one of them."

I focused on the small scar under her right eye—it was courtesy of Ronnie Calley. I wasn't the only one who had seen Peggy and Garrett on the washing machine that day.

"I think we'll be just fine," I said.

She snickered and ashed her cigarette. "It doesn't work out for the women of the MC. Look at your mom. Look at Ronnie. Cherry. Did it work out for them?"

"You left." I took a step closer and looked her up and down. "Did it work out for you?"

For once, Peggy was speechless.

I saw no point hanging around any longer.

"Like I said, I'm sorry about Isaac," I said.

As I began to walk off, she called out. "It's only a matter of time, Indy. He'll break your heart. Those Calley boys always do."

I didn't stop. I kept walking and disappeared inside where I continued to clean up. Peggy Calley was a spiteful, resentful, selfish woman. I wasn't going to let her words get to me, even if they were the echo of my own thoughts only a few weeks ago.

"You okay?"

I swung around at the voice. Chance Calley sat on a couch in the corner of the room, strumming a guitar. Seeing him brought a sudden rush of tears to my eyes.

"Chance!"

He stood up and pulled me into a big hug. I held on tight. Suddenly overwhelmed by the emotions of the day, and because seeing him again after all these years was so nice.

Letting him go, I couldn't help but smile. I'd always adored Chance. Growing up I always figured he was going to be a rock star because he was permanently attached to his guitar. In high school he could have any girl he wanted. Good looking. Charismatic. A talented guitarist. He'd surprised the hell out of everyone when he'd signed up for the Navy soon after graduation.

"I'm as good as I'm going to be, I guess," I replied. We sat down. "How are you?"

The years had done little to lessen his good looks, but he looked hardened—a little frayed around the edges. I knew being a Navy SEAL meant he was tough and fearless. But I didn't really know what it involved. Only that he saw a fair bit of action overseas.

He held up a glass of liquor from the table beside him. "Ask me after a few more of these." He tried to smile but his attempt was weak.

Across the room, Chastity Calley sat with her mom and Grandma Sybil. At nineteen, she was a wild beauty. Lashings of raven black hair fell around a porcelain white face that was pale in its beauty, and tumbled over her shoulders to her slender waist. Her large eyes, the same resplendent bright blue of her brothers and mother, were almond shaped and fringed with long, dark lashes. At the funeral, she'd sobbed into Caleb's shoulder. Isaac had been more like a brother than her cousin.

I turned back to Chance. "Did you make it to the funeral?"

I didn't see him at the church or the cemetery. But if he'd arrived late I could've missed him.

"Everyone was leaving when I arrived. I took four different flights to get here and not one of them left on time. I missed the service, but I got to say my goodbyes. I hung back with Caleb and Bull. Paid my respects." He took a mouthful of his drink, which smelled like whiskey. "I saw Cade ride off. Have you heard from him?"

I shook my head. "He needs time."

"Yeah, he does. He's not like you and me."

"What do you mean?"

"You're a trauma doctor now, right?" When I nodded, he put his guitar down. "We both stare down death every day. We watch it take those around us, indiscriminately. It teaches you a good appreciation of just how fucking fragile life really is, but at the same time, it almost anesthetises you."

"It still hurts when it happens to someone you love."

He sipped his drink again. "Sure. But I think facing off with death on a day-to-day basis makes you a little more stoic."

"Is that what you did overseas? Face off with death."

He drained his glass and plonked it back down on the table next to him. "Every damn day."

I thought for a moment. "Who do you think did this? I mean, do you think it was random? Or did someone want Isaac dead?"

"I don't know. Cade said he was messing around with H. Set up some rogue deal. Something like that would piss off a few people. Maybe it's a message for the Kings to keep our paws off their heroin trade." He picked up his guitar again and began to quietly strum it. "Whoever it was, they waited for the perfect shot and took it. He knew Isaac was going to be where he was; either that, or he followed him. And then he waited. Very patiently."

"What makes you say that?"

His eyes shot to mine. "Because that's what a sniper does."

"You think whoever killed Isaac is ex-military?"

"Maybe. It's hard to say. He's either really good and got in one shot that was meant for drama and a second to finish the job. Or he missed the first shot and scrambled to get a second in."

"Your gut feeling?"

His eyes found mine. "My gut feeling is that it played out exactly how Isaac's murderer wanted it to."

I stayed at the wake for a little longer, but when it started to turn real messy, I walked home in the rain and hoped that wherever he was, Cade was okay.

I arrived home, soaked with rain, and decided to take a shower. I stripped off in the bathroom and stepped into a deliciously warm stream of water. I soaped up my body, lathered my hair with shampoo and then conditioner, and let the heat of the shower wash away the tension and grief. Slowly, my muscles began to relax and I sighed.

Today had been heartbreaking. Isaac's funeral had been in stark contrast to my father's. Jackie Parrish had lived a lot longer, whereas Isaac was still young and strong, with a pregnant wife and a small son who was left behind. But he was gone. And I struggled to understand why.

When I opened my eyes, the door to the bathroom opened and Cade stepped in, his face and hair soaked with rain.

I watched him pull his shirt over his head, remove his boots, and the rest of his clothes. When he was completely naked, he stepped into the shower, and without a word, took me in his arms and pressed his mouth to mine. My body immediately responded and I melted against him, seeking comfort and pleasure in his hard body as it commanded me backwards until my back was against the wet, tiled wall. His big hands moved up to my face while his mouth moved fiercely over mine until his kiss left me breathless.

But his kiss petered out as his emotion overtook him. I looked up into his tormented face. Pain and grief were like shadows in his eyes. His face was stiff and I could feel his heartbreak radiating from him with every beat of his heart. He dropped his forehead to mine.

"I don't know how to do this," he said, his voice deep and strong, but at the same time, pained and heartbroken.

"It's going to be okay," I whispered.

He drew in a deep breath, his hooded eyes fixed to mine. "I don't know what I would do if I lost you . . ." His voice broke and his thumbs found the slick skin of my lower lip, his eyes intensely focused on it. I had only seen Cade cry once. When he was eighteen and he'd ridden all the way to Seattle to beg me to come back to him after we had broken up. Otherwise, he was

Penny Dee

fiercely stoic. But now, standing in the steam, he was barely in control.

"I'm not going anywhere," I replied.

His anguish was deep. I watched him squeeze his eyes shut and felt the slow exhale of breath as he opened them again. Droplets of water fell in rivulets down his beautiful face and dripped onto his parted lips.

His brows drew together.

"It hurts," he whispered.

I nodded. "I know."

He tried to kiss me but his lips trembled against mine and he pulled away. He slapped his palms against the tiled wall and took a moment. Water poured over his head and down his broad, muscular back. His face crumpled and he slowly sank to his knees, burying his face in my stomach. His fingers pressed deep into my hips. When I felt him shake, I knew he had given into his heartache and he was crying. I ran my hand through the wet tendrils of his hair, soothing him as he wept for Isaac.

I gave him a moment, and then slid to the floor beside him, wrapping my arms around him and holding him as he shook with the pain and grief of having to bury his best friend.

CHAPTER 6

CADE

I was determined to get to the bottom of why Isaac died.

I was going to look under every rock to find who was responsible.

The first person on my list was a ruthless thug called Saber. He was the president of The Knights, and if Isaac's death had anything to do with them and their bullshit heroin trade, then I was going to find out, one way or another.

And they would pay.

Once upon a time, I would've felt apprehensive about walking into The Knights' territory. Now I didn't give a fuck. I was so full of anger and the blinding need for revenge, everything else seemed so unimportant.

I rode up on my bike and pulled up in front of the clubhouse. When two prospects stepped in front as me as I went for the front door, I gave them a warning look. *Don't fuck with me.* I was there to speak to Saber, and I wasn't fucking leaving until I got what I wanted.

"You've got some balls turning up here with that fucking cut on, *pretty boy*," said a prospect with a huge chip on his shoulder and hair like a boy band member as he leaned in toward my face. I didn't move. Ten points to the kid for trying to be intimidating, but he needed to work on it. He was a joke.

"Nice try, kid. But either you step aside and take me to your president, or I'm going to show you exactly how committed I am to getting past you right now. And I ain't gonna lie to you, it's going to hurt you a lot more than it's going to hurt me. But make no mistake, one way or another, I'm getting inside that clubhouse and I'm talking to your president. Understand me . . . *pretty boy*?"

"I'll go get Saber," the other prospect said, quickly opening the door.

I didn't wait for an invite. I brushed past NSYNC and entered the clubhouse. It was dimly lit and opened up to an open-plan bar right off the front door. Three Knights in cuts were seated at the bar and turned around when I walked in, while the Knight behind the bar continued drying the glass in his hand. Across the room by the jukebox, a girl in barely there clothes wrapped herself around a scrawny looking dude with greasy hair and facial fuzz. They were drunk and making out between laughing and stumbling around the dance floor.

As soon as my cut became obvious to everyone, the vibe in the room dropped and the air was tight with tension.

"What the fuck do you think you're doing here?" One Knight growled as he came at me. He was my age, with scraggy hair and a patch on his cut that told me he was their SIA.

"I want to talk to Saber and I want to talk to him now," I demanded.

"Is that right?" The SIA looked around at the others in the room and laughed. "Pretty boy with the dimples wants to talk to Saber . . . *now*." He laughed and the others followed suit. But I said nothing, he could mock me all he liked. I didn't give a fuck. I just stared at him, my emotions slowly simmering beneath a dark look.

He stepped toward me and grabbed my forearm, pulling us together. "And what the fuck makes you think that's going to happen?"

I looked down at his hand on me, and then raised my eyes to burn directly into his. My words were slow, my tone low and dangerous. "Get. Your fucking hands. Off me."

He didn't move straight away. We were locked in battle and I could see he was weighing just how much of a threat I was to him. Slowly, his grip loosened.

"You've got balls coming in here, *King*."

I watched him let go of my arm, then I leaned closer. "You put your hands on me again and I will break every one of your fucking fingers. Do you understand me? Every. Single. One. Of them."

SIA laughed, but it was all bravado. His eyes betrayed him. He wiggled his fingers in front of my face and tried to laugh it off. "Ooooooooooh, scary guy."

I said nothing. But the look I gave him spoke volumes. I would take him down with no fucking hesitation if he got in my way again.

"Mind if I cut in, or is this a private dance?" came an amused voice from the bar.

It was Saber.

"Mind telling me why you've pushed your way into my clubhouse? Last I saw, this was a King-free zone." He gave me his legendary poker face. He was renowned for keeping the same expression throughout every situation. Happy, same expression. Angry, same expression. Stabbing you in the chest with a bayonet, same expression. It made him unreadable, and in the MC world, that was dangerous.

"I want to know who killed Isaac," I said.

He raised his eyebrows. "Isaac?"

"Don't pretend you don't know what I'm talking about. Who killed my cousin?"

"You mean that shooting outside of town last week? That was your cousin?"

"Cut the bullshit, Saber, you know it was. Tell me, was it payback?"

He stuck a toothpick between his lips. "Now why on Earth would there be a need for payback?"

"That's what I'm asking."

He held his arms out at his side. "It's all good, brother."

A noise from across the room interrupted us. We both turned to look. The drunk biker by the jukebox shoved his girl away from him and called her a whore. We watched as he smacked her to her floor and stood over her.

Anger ripped through me. "You going to take care of that bullshit?"

Saber shrugged. He didn't give a fuck. "Nah. I'm done here."

He turned and began to walk away.

The drunk biker hauled the girl up from the floor and smashed her in the side of the face with his fist, sending her stumbling against the wall. I was at his side in an instant, just in time to stop him from inflicting a second blow.

Gripping him by the collar, I thrust him up against the wall.

"Every part of me wants you to try that again. Just so I have the pleasure of stopping you." My voice was dangerously low and I had no doubt the look in my eyes let him know that there was no room for negotiation here. "You want to hit women, then you need to get past me first. Got it?"

Fury and frustration soared through me.

"Get the fuck off me," he spat.

"You like to hurt women?"

"Fuck you."

I smacked his head against the wall. My rage was a fucking freight train and it felt good having someone to release my fury onto. "You're a real douche, you know that? A really fucked-up piece of shit." I grasped his collar tighter and got real close to his face. "I see you hit a woman again, hell, if I even fucking hear about you hurting a woman, I am going to find you and break your goddamn face. Do you understand me?"

I released my grip on him and let him drop to his feet.

You would think he would walk away. You would think he would realize he had gotten away with it reasonably pain free and that walking away was in his best interest. But he didn't. Instead, he took a swing at me and it clocked me right in the eyebrow, splitting the skin open and sending blood trickling into the corner of my eye.

The fuckstick had pushed my last button.

And now I was going to have to hurt him.

It took three Knights to pull me off him. Then two of them held me back while one big mountain of a man called Hogg got ready to throw a few punches into me. But he was stopped by Saber's gruff voice in the doorway, commanding him to back down.

"Enough," he ordered.

Reluctantly, the thugs released their grip on me.

But I was already seeing red. *Blood fucking red.* So, as soon as I was free, I seized the gun I had shoved into the back of my jeans, and within a second, I was pointing it at them.

"Any of you assholes come at me again and I will kill you," I warned. And I meant it. I was done with being the nice guy.

Fucking done.

All three Knights took a step back. The woman-beater slumped in a bloody mess on the floor groaned as he slowly regained consciousness. Saber glared at me from the doorway. Unlike the other men, his body language was relaxed, unthreatened, because the fact that I had a gun pointed at them in their clubhouse was more disrespectful to him than an actual threat.

"You might want to think about what you're doing, Cade," he warned. "Such a show of disrespect can be very *unhealthy*."

"You tell these goons to keep their hands to themselves and I walk out of here." I gave him a pointed look. "With all my teeth."

He thought for a moment and then nodded at Hogg and his two sidekicks, before turning his gaze back to me. He folded his big arms across his chest. Along his forearm, amongst the collage of tattoos, were three thick, black crosses. Rumor had it, they represented the three lives he had taken.

"We are at peace, my *friend*. But if you ever come into my club and pull a gun on any of my brothers again, you won't be walking out of here in one piece. Me casa ain't no su casa. You got it?"

We stared at each other for a moment, his words hanging between us. I glanced at the girl shaking on the floor.

"She comes with me," I said.

Saber thought for a moment, his eyes dark and menacing. "You both leave now."

I walked over to the girl and hauled her up by her elbow, then turning my back on my rivals, walked out of the clubhouse and into the midday sun.

CHAPTER 7

INDY

I don't know what I expected when Cade returned. But him walking in with a busted-up girl from a rival club wasn't it.

I was in the clubhouse when the door opened and Cade swaggered in with the girl, Joker and Vader behind him.

"What's going on?" I asked as he walked toward me. I looked past him at the girl. Her face looked like she'd gone a few rounds with a brick wall.

"She needs medical attention," Cade said without looking at me. He made his way around the bar and dug a hand into the built-in ice bucket in the counter. I could read Cade like a book. He was angry at everyone and everything, and he wasn't going to bother hiding it.

I folded my arms and didn't move. "I can see that."

"Good. Then how about you see to fixing her."

I remained rooted to the spot. One eyebrow went up. "I'm going to need a little more information than that," I said bluntly.

Only now did Cade look at me. His usually sparkling eyes were dark and cold. "She's got a busted lip. A black eye—Jesus Christ, Indy, I'm not the one with a medical degree."

He pulled his hand from the ice bucket and wrapped it in a wet towel. But before they disappeared under the fabric, I noticed some very bruised knuckles. He'd been in a fight. Not with the mysterious girl— Cade would never touch a woman in anger—no, if I were to guess, I would say he got those swollen knuckles giving someone a taste of their own medicine.

Fine. I unfolded my arms. Because he had obviously helped save this girl from whatever had happened to her, I was prepared to let it go. For now.

I looked over at her. She was shivering. Not because she was cold, but because she was broken. And quite possibly drunk. Mascara ran in big black streaks down her cheeks and she wouldn't look at me. She simply wrapped her arms around herself and stared at the ground.

I offered a gentle hand to her shoulder. "Come on, honey. Let's get you cleaned up."

She looked at me with nervous eyes. Then they shifted to Cade, asking him for permission. But he was busy flipping the top off a beer, his mouth fixed, his jaw clenching.

"Come on," I said to her. "I'll get you fixed up."

Cade met my eyes and I matched his coolness with the coldest Arctic front a warm-blooded woman could pull off. The beer bottle paused at his lips as we passed by, and my eyes didn't leave his until we disappeared from the room.

"Are you really a doctor?" the girl asked as I got to work on her face with antiseptic cream and a Q-tip.

"Yes."

"Really?"

"What?" I asked. "I don't look like a doctor?"

She shrugged. "It's just, well… this is kind of the last place I'd expect to find a woman like you."

Sometimes I still felt the same way.

"That man…Cade. Are you his old lady?"

"No," I replied. But when I thought about it, that wasn't quite true. I was his old lady. We just hadn't said much about us to anyone. Because before we knew it, the reality of an MC life had pointed a gun at us and fired. Isaac was dead. Whether I was Cade's old lady or not seemed irrelevant. Unimportant. But now that I thought about it… yeah, I was Cade's old lady.

"You know, The Knights didn't have anything to do with that guy's death," the girl said, completely out of the blue.

"Oh, yeah? How do you know that?"

She hesitated and then leaned closer to me as if she was about to reveal a big secret. "They don't know it, but I overheard Saber and Hogg talking about it the other day. Hogg asked Saber if they were involved and Saber said no. Apparently, they have a big heroin shipment coming in from a new supplier and now wasn't the time to be starting any kind of melee with a rival club. He said they needed to keep their crosshairs on their new supplier and didn't need the distraction."

Once she started, she just couldn't stop. She was like a dam of secrets, all of them spilling out of her mouth. Listening to her go on, I thought about the MC saying: a scorned old lady can take down a club. And by the sounds of it, the loose cannon in front of me was heading in that direction. She knew things, she said. And she was going to make Clutch pay for hitting her.

"Saber and the club are deep in the local heroin trade. He knew about that dead guy's involvement with a heroin deal, but with the big shipment coming in, he wasn't going to make a move on it. Hogg asked him if he knew who killed him. Was it the Southern Sons or Satan's Tribe, and again, Saber told him no.

The Knights are heavily allied to the Tribe and he'd confirmed it with their president."

I stuck a Band-Aid over the cleaned cut. "There," I offered her a reassuring smile. "It's not going to scar."

The girl looked at me through her lashes. "Thank you."

"Can I call anyone to come and get you?" I asked.

She smiled. "I thought I might hang around for a bit. That guy out there with your old man. The one who looks like the lead singer from Faith No More, is he single?"

She was talking about Vader.

I shook my head. This girl wasn't going to learn. She needed to hop on a bus and hightail it back to Iowa.

But then, how could I say that when I was only getting in deeper myself.

CHAPTER 8

INDY

Two days later, after finishing up a day shift at the hospital, I drove straight home with a head full of plans for a romantic night in. Sex was non-existent between us at the moment, and I wanted it back. I knew Cade was hurting, but he was beyond preoccupied. He was obsessed, and I was going to bring him back to me. *To us.*

The house was empty when I got in. Not that I expected Cade to be home. He wouldn't be in until dinnertime, which gave me plenty of time to soak my aching muscles in a warm bubble bath and unwind with a glass of wine in readiness for the night's planned events. In my top drawer of our shared dresser was a brand new Victoria Secret outfit of white satin and the softest lace I'd ever felt. It was sexy. Indulgent. An invitation that was both blatant and carnal—the perfect wingman to help bring my man back to me.

After soaking in the luxuriously scented water for the good portion of an hour, I washed my hair and loofahed my skin to silky-smooth goodness, then climbed out and wrapped a big plush towel around me. I was big on moisturizer and had a ton of different bottles that I used regularly. Tonight's choice was a bottle of intoxicatingly arousing lotion that smelled both sweet and dark, with notes of pomegranate and sandalwood. It was sexy. Alluring. And I knew it would drive Cade wild as he covered my flesh with his warm kisses. Smiling to myself, I rubbed the perfumed lotion all over my naked body, the butterflies breaking loose in my stomach when I thought about Cade inhaling the scent off my skin as he crawled up the length of me.

Slipping into the lingerie, I had never felt sexier in my life. Hipster lace panties and a matching bra, I had never owned something so luxurious, so blatantly made to raise blood pressures and penises. And I felt excited just pulling it on and tying it up.

When six o'clock came and went, I checked my phone but there was no message from Cade.

The same with seven o'clock.

At seven-thirty I sat on the bed in our moonlit bedroom and felt the hurt spread through my chest. He didn't know I was waiting here in the dark for him, washed, moisturized, and wearing two hundred dollars' worth of lingerie. But it still stung.

I craved him so deeply it hurt. My blood buzzed through me and I lay back into the pillows and stared up at the moonlight streaming in through the window. My body was tight. I was so ready for Cade to come home and make love to me I could barely stand it.

As I thought about my big, strong, mountain of a man, I let my fingers trail down to the flat plane of my stomach and over the soft curves of my hips. Barely touching, they fleeted over the tiny strip of satin between my legs and drifted down the front of my thighs, sending tiny shivers through me. My nipples hardened and a throb took up between my thighs.

I hadn't planned on this, lying in the dark, bringing relief to the relentless wanting in my body, but I felt so tightly wound up, so tense with need. My hand drifted back up to my panties and my body flinched as the tips of my fingers delicately brushed over the smooth satin. Like gentle whispers against my flesh, my fingertips trailed back down to my thighs and up again, teasingly coming close to the tiny strip of fabric again but then stealing away. When I slowly brought them back and narrowed their area of focus to linger around my clit, my body lit up. I pressed harder and was rewarded with a delicious throb of pleasure and I moaned, thinking about Cade. I pictured him standing in front of me, gloriously naked with all his hard muscle on display.

In my head, his cock was in his hand and he was walking toward me, his face flushed with primal need, his eyes dilated with lust. When he approached me it was almost predatorily, like I was his prey and he was going to devour me, and I squirmed against my fingers with anticipation. When he reached me, I leaned up to him and ran my fingers over his thick chest and down his rippling abdominals, tracing the deep curve of his muscular V until I reached his big, swollen cock.

I bit down on my bottom lip as a surge of pleasure made the muscles between my thighs ache and clench with lust. I dipped my finger in and pulled it out again, swirling the slickness over my swollen bud of nerves. The tension was building. Rising. Winding me up so tight I was ready to burst.

In my fantasy I was on my knees, cradling my man's beautiful cock in my hands and sliding my tongue over the smooth head, teasing him with my lips and my tongue, and licking the pearly white pre-cum glistening on his skin. When I closed my mouth over him and took the length of him into my throat, his groan rumbled through me, his gasps of pleasure turning me on. *Yeah, baby, fuck my cock with your beautiful mouth. That's it, angel. You're going to make me come so hard.*

The muscles between my legs throbbed as I continued to toy with the swollen nub of my clit, building the tension. I wanted Cade inside of me, desperately. I wanted him to stretch me, penetrate me, and fuck me hard. I wanted him to flip me over and drive into me from behind. I wanted him to slam into me, hard and rough, so I felt every inch of him almost painfully hitting me in my womb. I wanted him to dominate me, overpower me, to fuck me to the point where I could stand it no more and I cried out his name as I climaxed. And then I wanted him to make love to me, painfully slow, every drive into my body purposeful and deliberate, every motion of his hips strong and controlled.

My body reacted at the thought and my fingers slid harder over my clit, pressing deeper, rubbing faster until all I was aware of was the rising pulse and surge of lust pumping through me to my very core. I teased harder, my temperature rising, my toes anchoring into the bed, my pussy growing slicker, more sensitive, and achingly ready to come. I bit down on my lip again and moaned, my breathing coming harder, my cheeks flushing as the tension finally erupted like a starburst and I climaxed. Ecstasy soared through me and my head fell backwards as I moaned into the moonlight room, my pussy pulsing violently against my palm, my spine arching in pleasure.

As I came down from my high, I started to laugh. My body felt so alive. So ready for my man. I felt flushed and drugged by my euphoria, and I wanted more.

It had been weeks. But tonight that was all going to change. Tonight when he came home I was going to bring him back to me. Bring him back to the present and make him see me. Touch me. Feel me.

As I caught my breath and my skin began to cool, my phone lit up with a message. I reached for it.

Cade: Don't wait up. I'm going to be late. Sorry, babe x

My happiness dropped to the pit of my stomach. Goosebumps spread across my skin and I felt a foreboding tingle at the base of my spine. The euphoria from my orgasm eddied away. The gap was widening. When tears burned in my eyes, I threw my phone across the bed and climbed off. Padding across the plush carpet of our new bedroom, I pulled on a silk robe and went downstairs. In the kitchen, I grabbed the bottle of wine, opened it, and stood at the counter as I threw back a decent mouthful.

I looked around the glossy white kitchen and drank in another.

Cade had given me this beautiful home.

But he was never in it.

CHAPTER 9

INDY

It had been three weeks since Cade had made love to me.

Something had changed in him and turned him to stone.

At first, I let it go. He needed time to deal with his emotions and get his thoughts straight. I understood that. But now . . . now things were getting ridiculous. Most nights he stayed up without me, training in his gym or sitting out on the deck under the stars, wrestling with the demons in his mind. On the nights when we did go to bed together, he would wrap his big arms around me and hold me against his strong, warm body. But it would never go anywhere.

I wanted to give him the space. He needed to get things right in his head and the last thing he needed was for me to be clingy. But enough was enough. It had gone on for too long and instead of getting better, it was getting worse. The distance between us was widening and I was beginning to wonder if we would ever find our way back to each other.

Rolling onto his side I curled into him and sought the comfort of his warm body next to mine. I inhaled the heat and scent from his skin and slid my hands down his muscular back and across his hips to settle on his warm stomach. I felt him stir. Felt our bodies start to respond instinctively and begin to shift against one another. I slid my hand to his boxers and Cade exhaled as I began to rub and caress him through the fabric. His lips parted and a moan escaped him. Lust pooled between my thighs. This was the most response I'd had from him in weeks and I was desperate for the drought to be over. Encouraged, I slid my hand beneath his shorts and felt for him, teasing him with gentle fingertips before wrapping my hand around him. He moaned as I stroked him, his cock throbbing against my palm as I did the things to him that I knew he liked.

With a hiss of breath, he rolled toward me, hoisting himself up with his big arms and putting himself between my legs and I immediately felt the hard ridge of his cock pressing into me. He kissed me hard, hot and desperate, his tongue penetrating me while his body moved urgently against mine. It was as if one simple hand job had kicked a hole in the wall around his heart and our kissing was bringing the wall down.

But then it stopped. Just as suddenly as it had started. He stared down at me, his breathing ragged, his cock still hard and pressing against me, his beautiful lips parted as he struggled to catch his breath. His eyebrows slammed together and I felt his breath leave him as he lost whatever war was taking place inside of him. He dropped his forehead to mine, and I knew our lovemaking was not going to happen.

"I'm sorry," he whispered.

When he looked away I turned his face back to me so I could look him in the eye.

"It's okay," I reassured him.

My body burned for him, and as he rolled away from me goosebumps tickled my skin. He left our bed and disappeared into the bathroom. Ten minutes later he came out dressed.

"Where are you going?" I asked.

"I can't sleep. I'm going for a drive."

I didn't fight him. There was no point. It would only push him further away. He needed time to face the demons inside him.

When I heard him drive off, I curled into my pillow and fought back my tears, wondering when my man was going to come back to me.

CHAPTER 10

CADE

I didn't know where I was going. I just needed to get out and drive. Roam the streets. Sometimes it felt like the walls were closing in and it scared the hell out of me because I didn't know who I was turning into. All I knew was a persistent need to find out who had killed Isaac.

I felt bad about Indy. She was reaching out for me, but I just couldn't reach back. And it made me feel even worse than I already did. She was my queen and I worshipped her, and there wasn't one ounce of me that didn't want to make love to her. But a black cloud had descended onto my soul and I found it harder and harder to block out the anger and grief to give her all of me.

Frustrated, I found myself down at the Playground—the local nickname for a part of town where streetwalkers sold their services to the johns who pulled up to the curb and asked how much. It was a busy part of Destiny. Here the air was thick with hormones, weed, and desperation. Sex was readily available. Whatever you liked. Hand jobs. Blow jobs. Traditional. Anal. Sex with toys. Twosomes. Threesomes. Any 'somes you wanted. For the right price, you got whatever you wanted at the Playground. It was the perfect place to find sex with no commitment, no false promises, and no expectation.

I pulled up to the curb where two women stood next to a streetlight and wound down the window.

"Hey, sugar baby, you looking for some company?" The redhead in a tiny pair of black shorts and a sparkly bra top asked. Her friend with a head of blonde curls turned her back to us as she lit a cigarette. The redhead winked. "No need for you to feel lonely tonight, baby. I can make you feel real good."

I leaned forward. "What about your friend? She available, too?"

The blonde swung around. She blew out a funnel of cigarette smoke as she sized me up. "You want a three-way baby, that's going to cost you."

"How much?" I asked.

"Three hundred," the redhead replied.

"Sure. No problem."

The blonde, who seemed a little more street smart and less of a performer than the redhead, cocked an eyebrow at me. "You show me the money, honey, and you've got yourself a deal."

I had twice that in my wallet. I pulled out six, fifty-dollar bills and showed them.

"Well, big boy, let's go party," the blonde girl said, dropping her cigarette to the pavement and crushing it with the heel of a thigh-high boot.

The redhead opened the backdoor while the blonde ran around to the passenger side.

"Ready?" I asked them.

The blonde snuggled up to my arm. "Yeah, baby, let's go do this."

"Are you for real?" the blonde girl asked as I pulled up out front of the diner. Her name was Nancy. The redhead was Rosie. "You seriously want to buy us a coffee?" She cocked a suspicious eyebrow in my direction. "Or is '*buy you coffee*' code for some weird-ass fetish you have?"

"Listen, ladies," I said, cutting the engine and turning to them. "As lovely as you both are, I don't want to have sex with you. I want to talk. That's all."

Before I could stop her, Nancy slid her hand over my crotch.

"Oh, baby, it don't feel like you just want to talk."

I wasn't hard. But she did cop a good feel of my cock.

I gently removed her hand.

"Coffee and food. How about it?"

They both thought about it.

"We still get the cash, right?" Rosie asked.

"Yes."

"The full three hundred?" Nancy gave me a suspicious look.

"The full three hundred, yes."

They both shrugged.

"Sure thing, baby. It's your money," Rosie said as she climbed out of the car.

Nancy waited and then leaned in, whispering in my ear, "If you change your mind, I'll fuck you for free."

After detaching her hand from my crotch, *again*, the three of us entered the diner. Rosie and Nancy both ordered pie and coffee, while I stuck with my black coffee.

"So, what's your deal, baby? Why's a hottie like you picking up girls off the street and taking them for coffee and pie in the middle of the night?" Rosie asked, digging into her apple pie.

Every time she moved, the bangles on her arms jangled and scraped along the plastic tabletop.

"Yeah. You look like you've got a lot going for you. Why you out here in the middle of the night paying two hookers to have coffee with you?" Nancy scooped up a big spoonful of pecan pie and devoured it with her perfect red lips.

I stirred my coffee. "My cousin was murdered."

Both girls stopped cold.

"Murdered?" Rosie spoke very slowly.

"By who?" Nancy asked, her mouth full of pie.

"I don't know. But I plan to find out."

"And how do *we* fit into it?" Nancy asked suspiciously.

The idea came to me when I was driving. The street. It was a giant network of comings and goings. People talked. People knew things. It was a source of information I hadn't tapped into yet, but I was going to start with these two.

"You both look like you're smart ladies. You know what's going on in every shadow of this town."

"Doesn't mean we know who killed your cousin," Nancy said.

"No. But people talk. And you ladies are in the . . . people business."

"What was your cousin's name, honey?" Rosie asked.

I had a feeling Nancy was naturally guarded and defensive, but Rosie could sniff out authenticity when it was sitting opposite her.

"Isaac," I said. It hurt saying his name. "Isaac Calley."

"The biker? He was a Kings of Mayhem, wasn't he?" Rosie asked.

I nodded.

"Does that mean you're a King?" Nancy asked, her eyes lighting up.

Again, I nodded.

Nancy sat back and toyed with her pie. "I don't know, man, I mean, I don't want to get involved in some biker showdown."

"You say that like you know another club was involved," I said.

She dropped her spoon on the table. "I don't know nothin' and I will deny anything—"

"Oh, shut up, Nancy," Rosie said. "Stop being so dramatic. He's only asking us if we've heard anything." Rosie leaned closer as if she was going to tell me a secret. "She's young and a bit of a drama queen sometimes."

"You know that I'm sitting right here, right?" Nancy said, picking up her spoon and poking at her pie again. "And that I can hear you."

Rosie didn't miss a beat. "See?"

I couldn't help but smile. Rosie was good-natured. Somewhere in her late thirties, her heavy make-up made her look a decade older. While Nancy, who couldn't be more than twenty-one, had an air of distrust around her.

"Does that mean you'll help me out?" I asked.

"Sure, honey," Rosie replied. "Whatever you need."

I looked at Nancy who thought for a moment and then rolled her eyes. "Fine. What do you need us to do?"

"Just keep your eyes and ears to the ground. If you hear anything about Isaac's murder you call me." I wrote my cell number on two paper napkins. "Anything at all. I don't care how meaningless it seems to you, if it's about Isaac's death, then you call me, okay?"

They both nodded. Rosie tucked the napkin between two massive breasts.

I stood up and put the three-hundred dollars, plus enough for coffee, pie, and a tip on the table. "Thanks. I know this wasn't what you were expecting. I appreciate it."

Rosie scooped up the money and started dividing it.

"Oh, honey, it's not the weirdest thing I've been asked to do tonight." She winked at me. "But it's certainly been the most delicious."

CHAPTER 11

INDY

Almost two weeks to the day of Isaac's funeral, another dark cloud descended upon the Kings of Mayhem MC.

I was in the ER when the call came through. A forty-five-year-old male. Head trauma and carbon monoxide poisoning. Found unresponsive. Resuscitated. Weak pulse.

When they rolled him in on the gurney I caught a glimpse of the Kings of Mayhem cut and my heart went into my throat. Dr. Burdett, our chief of trauma, took the case, but I followed them into Trauma Bay Two, a terrible foreboding creeping up my spine. Cautiously, I moved closer to them, not sure who was on the gurney—not sure how life was about to change.

Alarms beeped and the trauma bay came alive with an organized urgency as Dr. Burdett and his emergency team worked to keep the patient alive. When he flatlined, I heard the whirl of the defibrillator as it charged, followed by the three beeps to signal it was ready.

Dr. Burdett held up the paddles. "Clear?"

He placed the paddles on the chest of the patient and gave them juice. When the body on the table spasmed, that was when I saw him. *Tex*. His eyes were closed. His mouth slack. His face red. Another current of electricity ripped through his body, and he jolted, his body arching upwards and clenching, before collapsing motionless onto the gurney again.

Nothing. The heart monitor continued to show a flatline.

"Let's go again. Charge to two hundred," Dr. Burdett commanded.

Again, he applied the paddles to Tex's chest and sent another charge of electricity through to his heart.

Again, Tex jolted and then stilled.

Still nothing.

"Okay, let's call this one," Burdett said.

"No!" I said, stepping forward.

Burdett and his team looked over at me.

"I know him," I said.

One of the nurses spoke. "He was found unresponsive. He's been crashing the whole way here, Dr. Parrish. The chance of him having any brain activity left is minimal, at best."

Burdett looked at me for a moment longer, then turned back to his team.

"Charge it. Let's try again."

Again, the defibrillator charged and beeped. Again, Burdett sent another electrical current through Tex and into his heart. Again, I watched him jolt, flex, and then fall motionless to the gurney.

I closed my eyes. The nurse was right. The chances of Tex having any brain activity was unlikely.

"I'm calling it," Burdett said, snapping off his gloves. "Time of death 2:37 pm."

I felt rooted to the spot. Frozen by another death of a King in front of me. Burdett nodded at me as he walked past and disappeared from the room. Before I realized, I was alone with Tex. One minute the room was full of activity trying to keep him alive, the next minute, all the machines were disconnected and the room was cleared. *Tex was dead.* When I regained control of my feet, I approached him slowly. He looked peaceful—*dead*—but peaceful. Blood stained the pillow from a wound to the back of his head and his skin was red. Other than that, he showed no other signs of trauma.

"I'm sorry, Tex." I had known him for most of my life. When I was seven, he was a prospect in the club and he would play with Bolt and me in the treehouse when we needed babysitting. One time, when I was nine, he picked me up from school on his bike, and when he saw Joey Mattell teasing me he'd pointed at him and given him such a dark look Joey Mattell never teased me again. And when I had my tonsils removed, he visited me in the hospital and snuck in ice cream for me.

Now, he was dead.

My head lifted.

Cade.

How was he going to take this so soon after Isaac's death?

He was so tortured by his demons this could very well push him over the edge.

I reached for my cell but was interrupted by a nurse.

"Indy, you'd better come quick. I think some friends of yours are here and Dr. Burdett is about to deliver the notification of death."

"Oh, fuck," I whispered.

I ran through the ER and pushed through the doors to the waiting room, but stopped when I saw Dahlia, Ronnie, Bull, Caleb, and Cade all standing across the room. Dr. Burdett approached them, and before he even spoke Dahlia started to shake her head. I watched on, helpless, as she collapsed into Ronnie's arms and began to cry. Cade's eyes reached for mine and they were dark. His hands fisted at his side. His face stiffened with emotion. Next to him, Caleb exhaled deeply and ran his hands through his hair, while Bull contained his emotions behind his dark glasses. I was frozen to the spot, blood whirling in my ears, as the enormity of the situation crept up my spine.

Tex's death so soon after Isaac was going to devastate everyone in the club.

Slowly, I started to walk, my feet feeling heavy as I crossed the linoleum floor to where my friends, *my family*, rallied around Dahlia.

"I'm sorry, Dahlia," I said sadly.

Cade came to me and pressed his lips to my forehead.

"Are you okay, angel?" he asked, his voice rough.

I nodded and his big hands caressed the nape of my neck.

"They tried to save him," I said. "But it was just too late."

"If only I had gotten home sooner," Dahlia sobbed. "If only I hadn't stopped to pick up the goddamn groceries!"

I looked at Cade. His jaw was tight, his brows drawn. The news was beginning to take affect and I was worried about him. This was going to hit him hard so quick after Isaac's death.

Two days later, the medical examiner ruled Tex's death an accident.

After starting his car in the garage, he had left it running while he ran back inside to get something. On the way back to the car he had slipped and hit his head, knocking himself out. Unfortunately, he'd also fallen on the remote control to the garage door, closing it. Unconscious and unable to escape the exhaust fumes that quickly filled the small garage, Tex had died from carbon monoxide poisoning.

But I could tell by the look on Cade's face that he didn't believe it.

He didn't believe it at all.

CHAPTER 12

CADE

Chapel was a somber affair. The three empty chairs at the table were a grave reminder of the loss we'd suffered in the last few months. Sometimes I wondered if the damn club was cursed. So much had gone wrong lately.

Again, charters from all over the country descended on our small town for the funeral. We hadn't had a funeral in the club for almost eight years, but we were about to have our third in three months.

And I couldn't shake the feeling that we hadn't seen the last of the bad luck.

I felt helpless. Jackie had died of natural causes. But Isaac, he had been murdered, and the need to find out why was driving me to distraction. Now Tex was dead and I couldn't shake the feeling that it wasn't an accident.

It reeked of foul play.

Before Bull called an end to chapel, he stood up and dropped a patch on the table in front of me. Embroidered in white letters on black leather were the words *Vice President.*

The vote had been cast days earlier, prior to Tex's death, and the vote for me had been unanimous. I was now the VP of the Kings of Mayhem original chapter.

The room erupted with applause.

Bull put his hand on my shoulder. "We'll celebrate after we bury Tex."

We buried him the next day. He was laid to rest in a family plot in a cemetery just north of Humphrey. We buried him on a warm fall morning. There was the usual procession of bikes snaking down the highway with chapter flags flying in the cool Mississippi breeze. There was the service and the tears, and the heartbreak and everything that goes with the loss of a son, a father, a husband, and a friend.

As I watched his cut disappear into the ground, I wound my arm around Indy's waist, seeking comfort in the warmth of her body. When we were kids, Tex used to bring me Matchbox cars when he babysat me and my brothers. He taught me how to play poker. He snuck me beers at club barbeques when my mom wasn't looking. He endured a Britney Spears concert because Indy loved Britney and I loved Britney's boobs. He was there when I returned from Seattle without my girl and made sure I was okay when my heartbreak got too much for my sorry teenage heart.

Now we were putting him in the fucking ground.

My fingers twitched. Anger and grief crept up my spine and it was growing in strength. I was going to find out who did this.

And I was going kill them.

CHAPTER 13

INDY

The night of the lingerie incident, Cade had gotten in late, and when he had come to bed I had pretended I was still asleep because I wasn't ready to talk to him. I was hurt. Lonely. And I wasn't ready to push him to open up to me. I knew what it was like to lose someone you loved—it fucked with your head in ways you could never imagine—and I didn't want to push him away while trying to pull him to me.

But he was keeping something from me, and I wanted to know what it was.

Two days after Tex's funeral, I stood across from him in the kitchen of our new home, watching him drink his cup of coffee, and I was tempted to ask him about it. But I realized the likelihood of him telling me was zero to none.

So, when he walked out, saying he had things to do and wouldn't be back until late, and when he took his car and not his bike, I decided to follow him.

Now I was in my car in front of a diner halfway between Destiny and Humphrey, watching Cade escort two women inside. They sat at a window booth overlooking the parking lot. I watched them order, saw the waitress bring them coffee, saw both women light up a cigarette and Cade start talking. After a while, the waitress brought over two plates of pie, and while she was there she refilled Cade's coffee. The conversation seemed easy. There were no awkward pauses. No uncomfortable silences. Cade knew these women, and by the looks of it, this situation was familiar to him.

Climbing out of my car, I crossed the parking lot. When I walked into the diner and paused on the step, a small bell above the door alerted everyone to my presence. Cade sat with the women two tables down and all three of them looked up. If he was surprised by my arrival, then he didn't show it. He remained completely poker faced.

Straightening my shoulders, I walked over to them and calmly sat down, folding my hands in front of me on the table. Right away, the blonde woman widened her heavily made-up eyes and scoffed at me.

"Um, hello? This table is taken," she said. "You can't just—"

I shut her up with one look.

"It's okay, Nancy. This is Indy." Cade's eyes didn't leave mine as he spoke. "My old lady."

I raised an eyebrow at him.

And he raised one right back.

"You're his old lady?" Nancy gasped. She looked at Cade. "You're married?"

"As good as," he replied, his eyes remaining glued to mine.

"I think we should go," said the redhead sitting next to me. She stood up, the bracelets on her arms jangling as she stubbed out her cigarette and reached for her handbag.

"No need," I said, without removing my eyes from Cade. "You should sit down."

Out of the corner of my eye, I noticed the two women exchange a look before the redhead slowly eased back down.

"So," I said, cocking an eyebrow and tilting my head to the side. "What does a girl need to do to get a cup of coffee around here?"

CHAPTER 14

CADE

I don't know if I have ever loved her as much as I did in that one moment. Seeing her walk into the diner and calmly sit down at the table. Seeing how she hadn't mistaken this for anything other than what it was. She knew something was up, but she wasn't jumping to any conclusions. Not that I would blame her if she did. Especially with our past. But she didn't. My queen was fiercely loyal and now it seemed, fiercely trusting.

A smile tugged on my lips as I watched Rosie and Nancy. They looked anxious. Confused. Nancy seemed suspicious, while Rosie bit her lower lip and squinted her eyes as she scrutinized the situation.

We'd had pie once more since the first night we met, and again this afternoon. The second time we met up was because of an encounter Rosie had with a john who liked to talk while he jerked himself off over her huge breasts. *"Men are most vulnerable when they're coming,"* she explained. *"You'd be surprised by the secrets they let out with a stream of ejaculation."* Apparently, the talker was a member of the Satan's Tribe, a rival gang who ran out of Gulfport. He shot off his mouth as he shot cum all over her tits. He said their president—a Behemoth of a man called Balthazar—had arranged the hit on Isaac.

Armed with this information, Bull had dug deeper. Probed harder. Twisted balls. Found out the john was a wannabe club member who hung around the clubhouse like a bad stink, occasionally doing odd jobs for the club but never being drawn into the inner sanctum. There was no truth to what he said; he'd made up the story to sound like a tough guy. It was all part of his fucked-up fantasy.

Today I had asked to meet Nancy and Rosie because I was convinced Tex's death was no accident and I wanted to know what the word was on the street.

So far there was nothing, they said. No rumors. No gossip. No word.

They were just about to leave when Indy showed up and sat down. And I couldn't help but smile when my two very street-smart companions were knocked on their asses by one sharp look from my queen.

Amused, I watched as Indy listened to Rosie and Nancy explain our deal. They gave me intel and I gave them pie. That was it. Nothing else. Indy was calm. But I could tell she was angry with me, because I knew her. I knew the way she bit her bottom lip when she was trying to calm her thoughts. Knew the way she cocked one eyebrow when she was just keeping her temper in check.

I wasn't even sure what she was saying, I was too busy watching her, watching the way she talked to them, watching the way they took to her once they knew she wasn't a crazy old lady who wasn't going to rain hellfire and brimstone on them for meeting with her old man.

Because that was what I was. I was her old man.

And she was my old lady.

CHAPTER 15

INDY

The ladies left, leaving me and Cade alone. We sat across from each other, an electricity of unsaid words charging the air between us.

I waited for him to speak.

And he waited for me to speak.

"Okay, let me have it," he finally said.

"What do you want me to say?"

"You're angry," he said.

I nodded but spoke calmly. "Yes."

"I haven't touched those girls."

"I know."

His eyebrow went up.

I sighed. "I'm angry because you've shut me out. We're supposed to be together but you're turning away from me."

"There's nothing to tell."

Again, my eyebrow shot up. "You're secretly meeting with prostitutes. I think that's newsworthy."

"For no other reason than to find out what the hell is happening."

There was no need to rehash his reasons for meeting with Rosie and Nancy. They had been very straightforward in what they were doing for Cade. He needed them to be his eyes and ears on the street. He bought them pie.

"It's not just that," I said, my heart thumping in my ears. "There's a gap between us and it's widening every day."

He lifted his brows. "What gap—?"

"Don't pretend you don't know what I'm talking about." The fire in my eyes met the darkness in his. "I had to fuck myself the other night because you weren't there to do it. You're never there to do it."

"Jesus Christ, Indy." He shook his head and sat back in the booth.

I glanced around the room. Apart from a mom and her two kids down at the far end of the diner, and a lone lumber worker nursing a cup of coffee a few tables away, the diner was quiet.

"It's the truth," I said.

He shook his head. "We're not doing this here."

"Fine." I stood up. "We'll do it at home."

He stood up, too, and threw a couple of twenties onto the table.

When I walked away, he stopped me, gently placing his hand on my wrist. His eyes softened. "I love you, you know that, right?"

"That's not what this is about," I said, stepping away from his touch. "See you at home."

He followed me home in his car, and he was behind me when I ascended the steps to our front door. And when I walked into the kitchen, he was right there, behind me. I stood on one side of the island and he stood on the other. Two coffee cups left over from earlier still sat on the countertop between us.

"Do you blame me for not saving Isaac?" I asked, the idea suddenly occurring to me. "Is that it? Do you blame me for him dying."

Not that Isaac could have been saved. Even if his injuries had happened in a fully equipped ER, he would've still died.

"No!" he said.

"And Tex? Do you blame me for his death, too," I snapped.

"What? No!"

"Even though I wasn't the one who worked on him. I suppose it was my goddamn fault that he started his car before running inside to grab something. My fault he slipped and knocked himself out—"

"Stop it!" he said darkly.

"My fault he fell on the garage door remote so it closed, trapping him inside with all those car fumes —"

"Stop!"

"Well, it wasn't my fault. Just like it wasn't your fault Isaac was shot dead—"

"I said stop!" he yelled, slapping the coffee cup across the countertop and sending it smashing to the floor.

He was angry.

But so was I.

So I slapped the other coffee cup and sent it flying, too.

"You don't get to do this!" I yelled at him. "You don't get to blame me for Isaac."

"Blame you? I don't blame you. I blame me!" he roared, pointing to his broad chest. "It's *my* fault he died. It's *my* fault he was there. If I hadn't called him that night he would've still been sleeping in his bed."

"Isaac was killed because he was *fucking* with the heroin trade."

"No! He was killed because I was pissed at him and wanted to fuck with him by getting him out of bed at 2 am. Maverick was on callout with me. Not him!"

He fell forward, his palms slapping against the flat plane of the countertop.

"It wasn't your fault," I said with a shaky voice.

He squeezed his eyes shut and waited for the pain to subside. I could see his guilt had gotten the best of him. It had festered inside of him. It had been chewing him up for weeks, rotting his usual, easy-going nature.

"He wouldn't have been there if I hadn't called him," he rasped.

"If they didn't get him then, they were going to get him another time."

He looked up, his face pained and my chest was heavy with emotion when I saw the torment burning like wildfire in his agonized eyes.

"Isaac died because of me," he whispered.

"Stop," I said. "You know that's not true."

His fist pounded the countertop, veins as taut as ropes winding around his wide forearm.

"That's the thing, Indy." His throat worked as he swallowed. "It is."

He turned his back and began to walk away.

"Is that it?" I called after him. "Is that the reason you haven't been around? Or do you just not want me anymore?"

Cade swung back to face me. "What the fuck does that mean?"

"You haven't touched me in weeks. And the one time we do start to make love, you pull away from me and hide in the bathroom."

He brows shot in and his tight jaw ticked.

"I'm mind-fucked, in every way," he said darkly.

I shook my head. He didn't get to brush it off that easy.

"Stop pushing me away," I begged.

"I'm not," he said gruffly.

"If you don't want me—"

"Not want you?" He stalked back to me and grabbed hold of my arms. "You're the reason I fucking breathe!"

"Then why won't you let me back in?" I cried.

"Because I'm fucking terrified!" he yelled.

He let me go and took a step backwards, stunned by his own admission. His eyes were wild, his chest heaving, his mouth wet as he dragged his tongue over his lips.

"Of me?" I asked. "Of us?"

The emotion was bright in his eyes. His pulse thumped against his throat. As he ran his hand through his hair, he sucked in a deep breath to steady his nerves. Energy bounced off him.

"Losing Isaac broke my heart," he said, the agony in his voice as evident as the pain on his face. "But losing you would end me. Do you understand that? It would kill me."

I reached up and smoothed my fingers across his beautiful face. His admission slowly tempered our fight.

"I'm not going anywhere," I said.

"Neither was Isaac. Now he's dead." His face softened, and for the briefest of moments, he looked pained and . . . *tormented*. He turned away, his broad shoulders almost blocking the light from the window.

"I miss him," he said hoarsely.

We stood across from each other, only a few feet separating us, but the distance seemed much greater.

"Please don't push me away," I pleaded softly. Tears burned in my eyes. "I love you so much." I wrapped my arms around my waist and let the first tear fall. "Because I couldn't stand losing you for a second time."

CHAPTER 16

CADE

I turned away from the window and looked at my queen with her arms wrapped around her waist, and shame rolled through me. In my grief and guilt over Isaac's death, I had abandoned her because I was so distracted by my lust for revenge and my own self-loathing and blame. I had shut her out. I had hurt her. I hadn't touched her in weeks, and now she thought I didn't want her anymore. And why *wouldn't* she think that? It's what anyone would think.

Fuck, I was an asshole.

I was spinning out of control.

She was the most important thing in the world to me and I was torturing her every time I walked away from her. With every missed kiss. With every missed night in our bed.

My anger dampened and I went to her. I closed the space between us, and when she turned away, I turned her back to face me and lifted her chin so she had no choice but to look at me.

"There is nothing more important in this world to me than you," I said softly.

Tears slid down her cheeks and I gently wiped them away with my thumbs, feeling my own heart shatter with her pain. I bent my head to kiss her damp face. She exhaled deeply and I felt her body soften against mine.

"You're such an asshole," she whispered.

I held her face in my hands and pressed my lips to hers, opening her mouth with my tongue and taking command of her lips. She melted against me, but I could feel her anger and the hurt in her kiss and I hated myself for the pain I was causing her. Words weren't going to fix this. I was going to show her how I felt about her.

I wiped away a lock of hair from her face and looked into her big brown eyes.

"I'm sorry I've been shutting you out." I cradled her face in my hands and kissed the corner of her mouth. "I'm sorry for hurting you." I kissed the other corner. "I could live a million years and never deserve you." I slid my tongue between her lips teasingly and felt my longing for her take up inside of me. "But I love you so damn much it hurts." I thrust my tongue in and felt her melt into me. She moaned against my mouth and my body raged with need. My cock hardened as my fingers tangled through her hair and I kissed her hard until she was breathless.

When I broke away, I raised her hand to my lips and brushed them against the silver and turquoise band on her ring finger. It was the ring I had put there when making love to her on her return from Seattle.

"This should be permanent," I said.

She looked up at me and blinked away her tears. "Don't even think about asking me to marry you after you've made me cry."

A smile tugged at the corner of my mouth. Damn, she was cute.

I loved her so fucking much.

I pulled her to my chest and held her tightly, dragging in the scent of her deep into me. "What about after the orgasm I give you?"

She looked up at me and raised an eyebrow. "You haven't —"

I kissed the words from her lips and then pulled back, giving her a dark look. "Not yet. But I will."

The flame ignited and I lifted her up, my cock throbbing as she wrapped her lovely, long legs around me, and I carried her into our bedroom. And when we reached the point where my guilt about Isaac's death usually took over and dampened my desire with blame, I pushed it away until all I was consumed with was my desire for her. I took my time and removed her clothes, one item at a time, replacing them with kisses, until she was naked. She moaned restlessly beneath my touch, her fingers pressing into the nape of my neck as I moved lower, my tongue leading a damp trail down her warm body until I buried it in her slick and perfect pussy. Her hands dragged through my hair and lifted my head. Buried between her thighs, I had no choice but to look at her.

"Don't even think about stopping," she breathed.

I cocked an eyebrow at her. "Oh, baby, I have no intention of stopping."

With one lick into her slippery flesh I sent her head back into the pillow and a powerful moan rasped from her lips. Her hands tugged at my hair and her hips drove up to meet every lick as I fucked her with my tongue. And when I made her come, her thighs caged me in their warmth as she clenched and writhed in ecstasy, her fingers and toes curling into the sheets.

I rose up from between her legs and eased up her body, blanketing her in my heat.

"See," I growled, desperate to be inside her. "No stopping."

I kissed her then. Mindless with need. Wild with arousal. And because I couldn't wait one more minute to have her, I pushed deep into her, right to the very hilt, my cock throbbing at the sensation of her body tightening around me.

"I'm going to make you come until you beg me to stop," I warned, driving my hips into hers and snapping free from the chains of guilt I'd shackled to me for weeks.

She arched her back with the pleasure and dug her nails into my shoulders, her body squirming hungrily for me. I thrust into her again and again, my mouth devouring the moans escaping her lips. My body heated with lust and I was drunk on the sensation of her tight pussy gripping me, milking me, licking at the length of me. I grabbed her wrists and pinned her beneath me, rocking hard into her, losing myself in the bliss of bringing her to one orgasm after another. I kissed her jaw, her neck, the soft spot just below her ear, and felt her tremble beneath me. My body blanketed her, moving against her, grinding into her, my mouth and tongue fucking her mouth as I drove into her body, over and over again, until the tension burst and I came with so much force it blinded me. For a moment, I was suspended in nothing but euphoric white light where everything else but my ecstasy was gone. The world. Time. Everything. Simply gone as I floated in a blissful, ethereal light. I collapsed against her with a moan and sank into the mattress, my body drained, my mind delirious. I drew her to me and kissed her again, this time slow and leisurely, my head foggy and vague after such a powerful orgasm.

The heat of her body engulfed me and my eyes grew heavy. Beside me, I felt my queen relax and her breathing slow down. Entangled in each other, we slept, and for the first time in weeks I felt my entire body relax and my mind grow still. I don't know how long we slept for, but it was still light when we awoke and began to make love again. We lost time in each other. Neither of us interested in leaving the room. We fucked. We made love. We talked and kissed and fucked some more until our bodies were soaked in sweat and slick from our lovemaking.

When my phone started ringing I ignored it. I just wanted an afternoon where nothing but Indy existed. No pain. No grief. No psychopath out to destroy me and my brothers. Just me and my girl lost in our own little bubble of pleasure.

But as soon as my phone stopped ringing, it started again.

Again, I ignored it. Because Indy was sliding down my body, leading a trail of kisses from my chest to my stomach, her tongue sliding over the bumps of my abs as she made her way toward my cock. And call me insane, but no fucking phone call was going to interrupt what was going to happen next. Thankfully, my phone stopped just as she wrapped her perfect, full lips around the head of my cock and fuuuuuuck—I loved the way she gave head. Nothing, *no one*, compared to her.

When my phone started again, it was easy to ignore because my entire body was alive with sensation as the love of my life expertly fucked me with her mouth.

A fucking bomb could've gone off in that moment and I could not have cared less.

Except Indy cared. She ripped her mouth from my about-to-come cock and frowned at my ringing cell.

"I think you'd better answer that," she said.

"And I think you'd better finish what you were doing, baby, unless you want to give your man a serious case of blue balls."

When my phone stopped, she paused to look at it, then satisfied it wasn't going to ring again, resumed what she was doing, which was making me crazy with her lips, tongue, and her warm mouth.

When my pleasure rose I raised my hips to meet the torture of her mouth and she sucked me in deep, taking me right to the hilt. Indy didn't have a gag reflex, which meant she could take all ten inches without batting an eye, and damn, it felt good driving all of me into her mouth and into the back of her throat.

When my phone rang again, she tore her mouth off me in frustration and reached for it.

"No!" I breathed desperately. I was about to come. But Indy ignored me and handed me my cell. It was Bull.

"This better be fucking important," I snapped into the phone.

"Get your ass over to Irish's now," came his abrupt reply.

"It'll have to wait."

"You get yourself over here now. Someone shot Irish in the head."

CHAPTER 17

CADE

Irish was dead. His brains splattered across the wall he was slumped up against.

"What the fuck happened?" I asked Buckman.

"Would it mean anything if I said you couldn't be here?" he asked as he watched us walk into his crime scene.

The look I gave him told him no, it wouldn't matter.

We wanted answers and we weren't leaving.

He sighed. "Suicide. By the looks of it."

Bull and I shared a look of doubt. Granted, Irish held a gun in his hand, but it could easily have been placed there after someone had shot him.

This didn't make sense. Irish wasn't suicidal.

"Oh, for crying out loud!" came a familiar female voice. Bull and I looked up in time to see Sheriff Pamela walk in. She was the Sheriff based over in Humphrey. She gave Buckman a stern look. "Why don't you invite the whole goddamn town into the crime scene?"

"What are you doing here?" Buckman asked.

"You know the Watermelon Fields are considered No Man's Land," Pamela said.

She was right. Irish's home was in a part of town just past the watermelon fields known as No Man's Land. The area had been the subject of great dispute between the two towns of Destiny and Humphrey since the late 1800s. Because the towns were both located in different counties, it also meant No Man's Land fell under the jurisdictions of both county's sheriff's departments. I'd heard stories of the sheriffs flipping a coin to see who would take on an investigation.

"We were here first, Pamela. We were first on scene, so—"

Sheriff Pamela didn't give Buckman a chance to finish. Instead, she looked at us. "You boys know better than to creep around a crime scene. Now you skedaddle out of here."

Two nights ago, she had been on her knees in front of Bull. Neither of them would admit to what was going on between them, and it was amusing to see them pretend to not know one another when they were in public. The affair was a smudge on both their reputations. At first, it had been a one-night stand. But that one-night stand had been going on for weeks. Bull simply smiled at her, one of those secretive smiles full of promises about what he was going to do to her later, before he led me outside.

It was ironic to see Bull pussy-whipped by the police.

"What the fucking hell happened?" I asked him.

"Freebird and Irish had a disagreement back at the clubhouse last night. They left separately, but neither of them showed up this afternoon." He nodded to the prospect who was leaning against a tree, smoking a cigarette and looking a little grey. "The prospect found him about half an hour ago. Freebird is still missing."

"You think Freebird did this?"

"Things haven't been good with them since Jacksonville."

"I know. Freebird hasn't been able to let it go . . . but to do this?" I glanced over at Irish's slumped and bloodied body.

Had Freebird finally lost his head over what happened in Florida?

Bull knocked me on the shoulder. "Find Freebird. I want to know what the fuck went down after they left the clubhouse last night, and why he's been fucking AWOL all day."

I took one last look at Irish.

It was a question I wanted answered myself.

CHAPTER 18

CADE

The fallout from Irish's death, and the disappearance of Freebird, was massive. On the heels of Tex's death, and Isaac's murder only a few weeks earlier, the club was left reeling. We investigated. We probed. We made contact with some of the shadiest people we knew, but we came up empty-handed every single time. Either we were the unluckiest MC in the country, or someone had a vendetta against the Kings of Mayhem.

The tension was winding up inside of me, gathering speed with every death. I tried to train it out of me by hitting the gym every day, punishing my body until it was spent and fatigued. And when that didn't work, I threw myself into my work, mistakenly thinking that if I had control of everything else around me, then I would have control of my rising anger. My days were long. Demanding. And I would look forward to the end of the day when I could pull my queen into my arms and worship her body with every inch of mine.

But even the comfort of Indy's sweet kisses and sexy body couldn't keep the tension at bay forever. It kept building and building, winding up like a tightly coiled spring deep inside of me.

When Irish's funeral came along, I was so numb by all the death and loss, I was dangerous and I knew it. The funeral was another gathering of chapters. Another MC funeral where a cut was lowered into the ground, and another brother was honored with a celebration back at the clubhouse in true Kings of Mayhem style. But there was an undercurrent of distrust. A sinister entity simmering just beneath the surface. Some believed Tex's death was an accident, and that Irish had committed suicide. But they were the minority. Distrust hung like a thick layer of smoke over our club. I drank my whiskey, but not enough of it to numb me. After the fourth or fifth shot, I was done. I needed peace. I needed to be in the arms of my woman.

Indy drove us toward our home. And in my black mood, I just wanted to shut out the world and hold Indy close to me, and drink in the scent of her to calm my mind. There was no peace outside of her embrace and I was so damn tired.

It was late afternoon. Only a few other cars were on the road. My head was pounding. I needed sleep. Weeks of torment had caught up to me and my mind was dark.

My first realization of the beat-up truck was when it roared past us. I watched absentmindedly as it closed the space between it and the car in front, the pickup driver tailgating like a madman. He had my attention when he started to nudge at the bumper. He had my full attention when he rammed it and almost sent the car flying off the road.

I sat up straight.

"What the hell!" Indy said, watching the incident unfold in front of us.

"Slow down," I said.

"He's going to run that car off the road," Indy gasped.

I put my arm out. "Hang back, baby."

She slowed down to put space between us and the two cars in front.

With a third ram into the bumper, the car lost control and spun off the road. Instead of taking off, the truck came to a skidding halt next to it and a redneck with an axe climbed out. I heard the driver of the car screaming as the crazy redneck swung his axe down on her windshield.

"Pull over," I said to Indy.

She didn't argue and pulled over.

"Lock the doors and call an ambulance," I said. *Because when I'm finished with him, he's going to need it.* I felt the tension in me snap. I knew the bomb in me was about to detonate and I felt powerless to stop it.

The lady driver of the car was screaming for help as the wildman with the axe continued to smash her windows and her car, hollering at her about cutting him off in traffic. He was going to kill her, he said. He was going to fuck her up, he yelled, as he rained his axe down on her car, over and over again. She was terrified and crying, begging him to stop, holding her hands up in front of her face as glass floated around her like confetti.

I stormed toward them, and when the crazy redneck saw me coming, he casually turned his back and began to walk away. I continued after him. When he threw the axe in the back of his truck and opened the driver's door to climb in, I hauled him backwards, sending him to the ground. He got to his feet swinging, but I smashed my fist into his face and immediately rendered him useless. The second blow opened up his nose. The third broke it. Then I couldn't stop. The tightly coiled tension snapped inside of me and I continued to pound into him with my fist, my rage roaring out of me with all of my fear and frustration. With all of my hate and my pain. All of my agony. It boomed out of me like a missile. And I drove it into his face over and over again.

I was only vaguely aware of Indy saying my name and yelling at me to stop.

Slowly, my tunnel vision widened and the world around me came into view again. The redneck had gone limp in my arms, his face a bloody, pulpy mess. When I let him go, he slumped against his truck and groaned.

I looked at Indy. But she didn't need to say anything. The look in her eyes spoke volumes. I had lost control.

When the police and ambulance arrived, the deputy interviewed the driver and other witnesses, while the EMTs saw to the redneck.

"He saved my life," I heard the lady driver say to the deputy.

"I saw it," said another witness. "I think he would've killed her if that man didn't step in."

I watched them load the redneck into the back of the ambulance. He was going to be fine. But a few more to the face and he wouldn't have been.

"You come after another woman again and I'll finish what I started," I said to him before they closed the doors.

"That's about enough from you," the police officer said, dragging me away. "You're going to need to give me a statement."

Before I could answer, the lady driver came up to me and hugged me. Christ, she was only about nineteen. Probably a college kid.

"Thank you! You saved my life," she said, throwing her arms around my neck and hugging me again. When she turned to the police officer, she started to cry. "If he hadn't come along and stopped him, I think that psycho would've killed me."

"I'm taking him to the hospital to look at his hand," Indy said to the deputy. "You can meet us there."

I looked at her. "I don't need to go to the hospital."

But taking a look at my hand and judging by the pain that was beginning to burn in my knuckles, I had probably broken something.

The police officer looked at me from under the brim of his hat. "Good. I'll get the statement from you there."

Nothing was broken. In me, anyway. The psycho with the axe wasn't so lucky. He suffered several broken bones and a concussion, and Indy said he was being admitted. The police had already charged him at his bedside after a witness brought forward some footage they had taken of the attack on their cell phone.

Me, I wasn't being charged.

But I should be. I had lost control.

I knew it.

And worse, Indy knew *and* had witnessed it.

She hadn't said anything, but I knew it weighed on her mind.

She was quiet as we walked down the corridor of the hospital, leading outside, and I wanted to talk to her about it when we were alone. But just before we walked through the door, someone called my name.

"Mr. Calley!"

Indy and I swung around. Dr. Sumstad, the county medical examiner, approached us from the opposite end of the corridor.

"Those toxicology reports came back on your friend, thought you'd like to know before I hand my findings over to the proper authorities," he said as he walked toward us.

The donation to Sumstad's kid's Boy Scouts fund let him know that yes, the Kings would like to know before anybody else got their hands on the findings.

He handed them to me, but I had no idea what the hell I was looking at so I gave the papers to Indy. Her eyes roamed over the report.

"What did you find, Dr. Z?" I asked.

"Apart from significant levels of THC, nicotine, and alcohol, no other drugs were found in his system. If he was taking medication for depression, such as SSRIs or TCAs, then he hadn't taken them in days." He nodded to the file in Indy's hands. "What I found particularly interesting, though, was Mr. O'Connor's blood alcohol level was .455."

"Jesus!" Indy exclaimed.

"His levels were four times the legal driving limit," Sumstad said.

"Meaning?" I asked.

"Meaning, Irish was too wasted to stay awake, let alone make the decision to put a gun in his mouth and pull the trigger," Indy said.

"Exactly," Sumstad agreed. "Also, his brain stem was severed by the bullet. But the police report said he was clutching the gun in his hand when he was found."

I didn't know what that meant, so I looked at Indy.

"The moment the brain stem was severed, it became an anatomical impossibility for him to maintain a grip on that gun."

"Precisely. So, based on this, I'm citing cause of death as homicide."

CHAPTER 19

INDY

We lay on our bed in the darkness, the only light in the room coming from the streetlight farther down the road. We were awake but still. Lying together but not touching. Saying so much but not uttering a word. Emotion buzzed around us. We were showered and changed, me in a t-shirt and bed shorts, and Cade in a pair of sweat pants hanging low on his hips, his broad chest naked. We lay on our sides, facing each other. Our heads sank into pillows. Cade was calm, but shame clouded his handsome features.

"I scared you," he whispered, his throat working as he swallowed. "I saw it in your eyes."

The torment was clear on his face, and my heart ached at the sight of it.

"You didn't scare me," I whispered back. "But you were out of control."

His eyes didn't leave mine. They were dark and blue, and full of turbulence.

"I don't know if I would've stopped. The pain . . . the anger . . . I couldn't hold it back any longer," he said and I could hear the anguish in every word.

"But you did."

"Only because you stopped me." His brows drew in. "I don't know what I would've done if you hadn't."

"You would've stopped," I reassured him.

"Do you really think so?"

I nodded gently. "But I don't live my life with *what ifs*. I think if you're concerned, then you should speak to someone."

He chuckled softly. "Spoken like a true doctor."

"Counseling is for big bad bikers, too," I teased softly with a playful raise of an eyebrow.

That was when Cade opened up to me and told me about seeing a psychologist after I had left for college. How his counselor, a sincerely nice guy named Donnie, had helped him cope with his emotions through counseling and journaling. I let him speak without interruption, and it all spilled out of him. About the desperation he'd felt after our breakup and his inability to cope with the loss of our relationship. How he had struggled with his father's death less than a year later. And then with Donnie's death in a car accident not long after.

I reached for his bandaged hand and brought his fingertips to my lips.

"I've got you," I said softly, pressing a kiss into them. "And I won't ever let you go."

His eyes roamed my face, absorbing what I had said and looking for signs that I meant it. He reached up and tenderly pushed my hair from my face, tucking it behind my ear.

"Will you marry me?" he asked quietly.

I nodded gently.

"Yes," I whispered.

His smile was tender, barely showing on his face, but registering brightly in his beautiful eyes. "I don't want to wait. I want you to be my wife as soon as possible."

I curled my fingers around his. "And I want to be your wife more than anything in the whole world."

He linked our forearms together and held them to his chest, and I could feel the gentle thump of his heart. When he bent his head and kissed the top of my hand, I was consumed by love for him.

"Do you want a big, white wedding?" he asked.

I shook my head. "No. I just want to be married to you. I don't care how we do it."

And it was true. I wasn't a white wedding kind of girl. I'd never fantasized about a wedding. Because I had already had it when I was nine years old, when I had married my best friend in the backyard, in front of my brother Bolt.

I smiled and pressed my forehead to his. "Plus, we already had our big wedding when we were nine, remember?"

He laughed softly, barely a whisper, but his smile was warm. "I love you so much, Indy. Please don't give up on me."

His words killed me. I reached up and cupped his jaw with my hand, and kissed his beautiful lips. He was a big man. Physically powerful and broad. He was tall and intimidating, strong and protective in every way. But in that moment, he needed me. He needed to know that I was standing beside him through everything, no matter what. And it killed me to know that he needed that reassurance. Because he had it. No matter what happened. I would rise up as his queen and stand next to my king. "I will never give up on you . . . on us. I've got you, baby. Whatever you need from me. Whatever I can do. Whatever I can give you. It's yours."

I felt his breath leave him. Felt his body relax.

We didn't make love. We just held each other, united by the emotion in the room. He drew me into his arms and held me against the warmth of his chest, his fingers trailing up and down my arms in blissful whispers. And I made a silent vow to this man. To always stand proudly by his side through every storm, and to love him with every beat of my aching and abundant heart.

CHAPTER 20

CADE

The party to celebrate my vote in as Vice President was held a week later and it was huge. Some bikers from visiting chapters lingered for the party at the clubhouse. Bull was adamant the celebration went ahead because we needed something good to bring us all together, rather than a fucking funeral.

The vibe was good. Everyone was ready to celebrate. To be happy. To put the grief behind us and have a good time. A live band played. We had caterers bring in a spit roast with roast potatoes and all the trimmings. Bourbon flowed. Tequila was shot. Weed was blown. Coke was racked up and enjoyed.

But for me, I stayed clear of it all.

So did Indy.

Because after Bull made the announcement and formally swore me in as VP, and when he asked me to make a speech, I changed the course of the night.

"We're all here to celebrate me becoming the VP of this club," I said into the microphone, and the room rumbled with cheers.

"But that's not the only thing I want you to help me celebrate tonight."

I looked across at Indy. She was standing with Abby and Mirabella, looking beautiful in a short white dress with a plunging neckline and a choker of daisies around her milky white throat. She looked stunning and my heart overflowed with love for her. In a room full of leather and liquor, lace and smoke, she was an angel. I offered my hand to her and she stepped up onto the small stage to join me.

"Because tonight, I'm going to make this beautiful woman my wife."

The room vibrated with surprise, and the applause that followed shook the walls.

A marriage celebrant from town joined us on stage. And as we stood there in front of all of our friends and family, I looked over at the woman who meant more to me than the air in my lungs, and a peaceful calm washed over me. I could withstand anything if she was by my side. And when I draped the custom-made crown necklace I'd gotten for her when I was seventeen, over her neck and made her my wife, it was the singular, happiest moment in my life. Indy was mine. All mine. *Finally.* I took her beautiful face in my hands and kissed her, and the room erupted in celebration. But they all faded away and went out of focus as I continued to kiss my wife, lost in the moment of finally becoming her King.

"I love you so much," I whispered against her lips. I felt her smile and pull me closer, her reluctance to end our kiss as strong as mine.

Afterwards, we celebrated with our family and friends, and the festivities rolled on into the night. It was the first time in months that we were able to forget, just for once, and no one was ready for it to end. We danced. We drank. We ate. We laughed. There was a feeling of freedom in being able to let go and forget. Some of my club brothers celebrated a little too much, and toward the end of the night it got wilder. Louder. Crazier.

But I was so lost in my queen that I never left her side. And as Paula Cole's

"*Feelin' Love*" played on the jukebox and I held her in my arms, I looked down at her, aching to be inside her.

"Time to go to bed, Mrs. Calley?" I bent my head and nuzzled into her throat, dragging my tongue up to her ear. I was done waiting.

She shivered beneath the caress of my lips against her skin and a soft moan left her parted lips. "Please," she breathed.

We arrived home, and I scooped her up in my arms and walked her across the threshold because it seemed like the right thing to do, and carried her straight up the stairs to our bedroom where I wasted no time peeling her clothes from her body. We fell onto the bed, kissing furiously, neither of us wanting to wait a moment longer. I moved between her thighs where she was slick and tender, and a tremor rippled through her as I pushed into her. She gasped and clenched around me, moaning my name as I slowly pulled back, only to thrust back with more force. Her head fell back and her fingers pressed into my shoulders. I drove into her, over and over again, my cock feeling so fucking hard it was almost painful. And I lost myself in the noises she made, in the moans and the whimpers, in the soft, tortured pleas for more.

I was making love to Indy and she was my wife.

My wife.

I started to come, and my groan was long and drawn out, syphoned out of me by an orgasm that was equally as powerful as it was euphoric. I gripped at the sheets beneath her and buried my face in her hot, slick neck, overwhelmed by the pleasure as I jetted hotly into my wife.

When our breathing eased, I rolled onto my back and drew her into my arms, kissing her forehead. It was 5 am, and outside a hint of pale light was breaking over the treeline as dawn slowly began to rise above the town. It was the beginning of a new day.

And for us, it was the beginning of our new life together, finally, as husband and wife.

CHAPTER 21

INDY

Two weeks after we got married, I was finishing up a day shift at the hospital when one of the nurses told me Mirabella was in the waiting room asking for me.

After I finished with a twenty-five-year-old who had managed to break one of the trickiest bones to break in his hand doing some weird sex act even Tito would raise his eyebrows at, a nurse led Mirabella into the cubicle where I was typing up my notes. I greeted her with a warm hug.

"What a wonderful surprise," I said. "But I'm anticipating this isn't a social visit."

Mirabella beamed. "I think I'm pregnant."

"You do? That's wonderful."

"I've been feeling a bit strange now for a few weeks. And my period is late."

"That's a good indication." I smiled. Jacob and Mirabella were going to make beautiful babies. "Well, let's find out, shall we?"

While Mirabella visited the bathroom with a sample jar, I checked my phone. Cade had sent me a message.

I'm taking you to dinner.

I smiled as I sent one back.

Do I need to change first? I'm in work clothes.

He texted me back straight away.

The sexy doctor look turns me on. I'll take them off you later. See you soon.

Mirabella reappeared and handed me her urine sample.

"I'm trying not to get my hopes up," she said, taking a seat. "But I can't wait to give Jacob a baby."

"Are you trying?" I asked as I stood at the cubicle bench and tested her urine.

She nodded. "We want a big family. I'm an only child and Jacob grew up in foster care. He never knew his parents and he never stayed in one place long enough to really feel like he belonged anywhere." She laughed, a beautiful but nervous laugh. "Listen to me carrying on like garrulous fool. I'm nervous, I guess."

I held up the pregnancy test and grinned.

"Is it positive?" Mirabella asked, calmly.

"Yes. It's positive."

"I'm pregnant?"

I nodded and she stood up and came toward me, and pulled me into a big hug. "Thank you!"

I laughed. "I swear, I had zero to do with it."

"I'm so happy," she said, her face bright with joy.

"I'd like to do a quick ultrasound, see how far along you are."

Mirabella agreed, and ten minutes later the grainy black and grey image of her baby appeared on the ultrasound machine. I rolled the transponder over her slick belly so I could see her womb from different angles.

"You're actually quite far along," I said, clicking a button to record the image. "You're almost fourteen weeks."

"Fourteen weeks!" She laughed. "I guess I was so caught up with the wedding preparations I didn't notice how late my period was. And I've only really started to feel different in the last few weeks. I did have some spotting a few weeks ago. I thought it was a light period. Is that normal?"

"It's quite common. Did you experience any pain?"

She shook her head. "Very minor. Does that mean there is something wrong with my baby?

"Everything looks really good," I reassured her. I moved the transponder around her belly, pressing it in deeper just below the bikini line. "Do you want to know the sex?"

She looked surprised. "You can tell this early?"

"Yes. And you're little one seems quite happy to let you know."

Her beautiful face broke into a smile. "Yes. Please. I want to be able to tell Jacob if he is having a boy or a girl."

"Do either of you have a preference?"

"No. We just want *our* baby. A little human made up of the two of us."

"Well, you can tell Jacob he is going to meet his daughter in about six months' time."

"A girl?" Mirabella whispered.

"Yes. You're pregnant with a baby girl."

After cleaning her belly and redressing, Mirabella pulled me into another big hug. "I'm so happy. Thank you."

"I'm guessing you're dying to tell Jacob?"

"He dropped me off. I told him I had a female situation that I needed your advice on, that way he wouldn't ask too many questions. You only need to mention the word menstruation or tampon around him and he turns green."

"Well, I've finished up here, so I'll walk out with you." I handed her a few pamphlets on pregnancy. "Give me a couple of minutes to sign out and I'll grab my bag, okay?"

Five minutes later, we walked out into the late afternoon sun.

"How are you going to tell him?" I asked, enjoying the buzz of Mirabella's happiness.

She linked her arm through mine. "I'm going to take him home and make love to him. Then I am going to sit him down and very calmly tell him that our life is about to change." Her smile was bright and her glorious hair shined in the hazy golden light of dusk. "I'm so happy, Indy. I don't even know the words."

"I'm sure Jacob is going to feel exactly the same way," I said.

"Speak of the devil," Mirabella said, nodding toward Jacob and Cade who were walking up the road together. She waved to her husband who grinned back at her. "He doesn't even realize that his life is about to be turned upside down."

That was the moment everything changed. The moment when everything slowed down and happened in a blur.

I heard the sound of the bullet as it ripped through the air and thrust into Mirabella's forehead. I saw her eyes widen and then go vacant as her body went limp. I grabbed her to stop her from falling, but the weight of her lifeless body dragged us both down to the sidewalk. I felt the thud of the pavement beneath me and the scrape of my skin against the concrete. I looked up and saw Cade and Jacob pause on the pavement, and then all of a sudden sprint toward us, Jacob's face twisting in terror as he bounded along the street. When he reached us, he fell to his knees and grabbed his wife, crying as he tried to scoop her skull up from the concrete and piece her head back together again.

Cade tried to shield me from the invisible gunman. He ripped his gun from the back of his jeans, scanning the buildings that towered above us. It was like everything was happening in a vacuum where there was no sound. Everything was slowed down and muted. Blood whirled in my ears and my brain spun, trying to understand what had just happened in the silent scene unfolding before me. Then, quite suddenly, the sound returned and Jacob was screaming, and screaming, his heartache spilling onto the sidewalk like the blood from his dead wife's open skull.

People ran toward us from all directions, and Cade shoved his gun back into his jeans. He crouched down, his face pale, his eyes bright.

"Are you hurt? Indy, are you shot?"

I looked at him, dazed and confused, and shook my head. I tasted the familiar metallic taste of blood on my lips but knew it wasn't mine.

Suddenly, there were so many people. So many. But I felt too stunned to move. Jacob pulled Mirabella from me and cradled her in his arms. He petted her face as he cried, and clutched her motionless body to his chest. Her eyes were half-open and dull, staring unseeing out at a world that had erupted into chaos. With a sob, Jacob pulled her tighter to him, and her arm slid free and fell limp to the concrete.

Mirabella was dead.

Cade pulled me into his arms, and even in my stupor I knew it was so he could protect me from any more bullets.

A siren broke into the confusion. I raised my shaky hands to my face, they were covered in Mirabella's blood and all I could do was stare at them as I slowly descended into shock. Cade held me tight. "It's okay," he said. But he was wrong. It wasn't okay.

Someone had just shot Mirabella and her unborn baby dead.

CHAPTER 22

CADE

That night, a melancholy descended on the club.

Mirabella's death shook us all. Bull called a lockdown the moment he heard about the shooting, and everyone immediately associated with the club was ordered to the clubhouse. For the night, at least. Club members. Wives. Girlfriends. Kids.

Extra security detail was called in to protect the club.

While the old ladies and other family members united in the clubhouse, Bull called chapel. All OC members, plus a few charters still lingering in town from Irish's funeral, were in attendance. Except Jacob. When the police had tried removing Mirabella's lifeless body from his arms, he had really lost his shit. He'd fought them off with his fists, his strength, and finally, his Glock. It took three cops to take him down and an EMT to sedate him. Now he was sleeping it off in St. Gabriel's.

Fuck.

A few inches.

That's what I struggled with more than anything. And I felt like a real dick. But a few inches to the left and it would've been Indy lying dead on that sidewalk and me sleeping off sedation in the hospital. The thought made me sick. I banged my fist against the table and the sound reverberated through the room. Talking stopped.

"We're under attack," I said, my teeth gritted and nostrils flared. "For whatever reason. Someone is out to hurt the club. Isaac. Irish. Now Mirabella. And Tex, too. There is no way his death was a fucking accident."

"Buckman said the FBI are now involved," Bull said, and the room rumbled with the response of twenty-three Kings and their opinions about law enforcement.

"Pretty quick of them to get involved," Vader said.

"They're saying Isaac and Mirabella's deaths are serial killings." Bull turned his head in my direction, but he had on his glasses so I couldn't see if he was looking at me. "They'll look into Irish and Tex."

"So we just wait around pulling our dicks until they do something?" Cool Hand asked.

"I'm sure law enforcement will be all over the murders of three bikers and an old lady," Griffin added sarcastically. Since Isaac's death he seemed to have aged another ten years. "I want justice for my son. For Irish, Tex, and Mirabella."

"And you'll get it," Bull said calmly. "We'll find our own justice. But first we need to piece this shit together. Work out who has the motive."

"What about Freebird?" Elias said. "Is there a chance he's involved?"

"I'll pretend you didn't say that," Maverick said, giving Elias a murderous look. He and Freebird were tight. "Freebird is a brother."

"But he is also missing," Joker said, ignoring the look of wrath from Maverick. "You can't dispute that."

"And he's ex-military," Elias added.

"Half the goddamn club are ex-military." Maverick's nostrils flared. "Freebrid isn't responsible for any of this."

"Then where is he?" Joker asked.

Maverick stood up. "Asshole!"

Joker stood up and the situation spiraled out of control because tensions were high.

"Enough!" Bull demanded from his chair at the head of the table. "Sit the fuck down. Both of you." He removed his dark glasses and his bright blue eyes narrowed against the light. "Cade is right. Someone has got a beef with this club. Now instead of puffing our chests and letting our emotions get the better of us, let's work this fucking thing out!"

CHAPTER 23

INDY

I was in shock. Devastated. I had seen people die in front of me many times, but watching Mirabella die knocked the wind out of me.

While Cade went to chapel, I went to the roof. It was out of bounds, but I needed the space because we were two hours into lockdown and already the walls were closing in on me. I needed to escape the other women and find some comfort in solitude.

I sat down on an old deck chair and stared up at a starless sky. The full moon was too bright for stars and it bathed the night in bright white light. I sank back into the chair and lit up the joint I'd scored off of the prospect. I closed my eyes and let my emotions rise to the surface. Today I watched a beautiful young woman, who was pregnant with her first baby, get assassinated by an invisible evil out to destroy the club.

"Indy?"

I opened my eyes and turned my head. It was Elias. He looked apologetic.

"I'm sorry, but you can't be up here, ma'am."

I didn't say anything but instead offered him my lit joint. He shook his head. "No, ma'am."

I shrugged and took a toke, dragging the sweet-scented smoke deep into my lungs. "Whatever floats your boat," I said, slowly exhaling the funnel of smoke. "But for fuck's sake, stop calling me ma'am."

Elias looked uncomfortable. I liked him. He had gentle eyes and he was always very kind.

"I'm sorry to wreck your solitude, Indy. But you really can't be up here. Cade won't be pleased if he finds out. Chapel is over. He'll be looking for you."

Cade's need to protect me was only going to ramp up after this. I would be lucky if I got to go anywhere without an armed escort again. I had seen the look on his face and the fear in his eyes when we had given our statements to the police. Only a few inches over and it would have been me dead and cold on the medical examiner's slab. That fact hung silently between us during the car ride home, and I knew Cade's fear had taken a sharp shove into terrified.

I rolled my head to face him.

"Have you ever lost anyone, Elias?" I asked.

He thought for a moment, hesitated, and then nodded. "Yes, I have."

I took another drag on the joint. "Want to tell me about it?"

He shrugged a little. "Nothing really to tell. My sister died some years back. Then my mom and stepdad."

I blew out the smoke. "It hurts."

He nodded.

"I lost my brother when I was twelve. Then my daddy. Now Isaac. Tex. Irish. Mirabella . . ." I let my sentence slip away. The smoke was starting to take affect and I was feeling calmer. Numb.

"What gets me is that there are so many assholes out there who just float through life with all their fuckery and nothing happens to them. They just float on by doing whatever ghastly deeds they want. And nothing fucking happens to them." I closed my eyes against the image of Mirabella being shot and collapsing in my arms. "But then you get an angel like Mirabella—" The words choked in my throat. The emotion rose up from deep within me and lodged in my windpipe.

Elias looked around us and then crouched down beside me. I offered him the joint again, and this time he accepted it.

"I heard you were with her when it happened," he said, taking a drag and holding it in before letting it out in a cloud of sweet smoke.

I exhaled deeply and nodded, my body flooded with grief. "Yes."

"Did she say anything?" he asked softly, handing the joint back to me.

I shook my head. "It happened too quick. We were just walking and then . . . the bullet went straight between her eyes. Killed her immediately."

Elias exhaled deeply, and I could see by the look on his face that he was affected by it.

"Jacob is going to take this hard," he said. "But we'll do everything we can for him, Indy. And you."

I could still hear Jacob's cries as he tried to piece his wife's head back together. A wash of sadness spread across my skin, and I let out a deep breath of heartache.

"Thanks, Elias. You're a good guy."

"Thanks." He smiled and gave me a wink. "But I won't be if your old man finds you up here. How can I convince you to go back inside?"

"It's alright, Elias." The voice with an edge to it came from behind us and we both turned to look. It was Cade. He'd made it onto the rooftop without being heard. "She's not going to listen to you. I got this."

Elias stood up and gave me a wink. "Stay safe, okay, Indy."

After he left, Cade pulled a crate over to where I was sitting and sat down.

"I know you don't like being told what to do, but, Indy, we're in lockdown—"

"Want some?" I cut him off, offering him my joint. I didn't need the safety speech. I needed to be numb.

He shook his head. "I can't protect you if you do things like this."

"Come to the rooftop for a joint?"

"We don't know who is doing this, Indy. Who they are. Where they are. You can't be out here, exposed."

"We can't stop living our lives."

"No. But we can take precautions." His face softened. "Baby, work with me here. You're my number-one concern. If anything happened to you—"

"I get it. I'm sorry." I reached for his hand and squeezed it, exhaling deeply as I fought back my tears. I slumped back into the chair. "She was pregnant."

Cade's eyes widened, just for a moment, then settled as the realization set in. His jaw tightened. "Jesus Christ," he growled, running his hand through his hair. "Does Jacob know?"

I shook my head and finally my tears broke free and spilled down my cheeks. I didn't want to think about Jacob finding out. It would kill him.

Cade scooped me up and held me against his big chest, and I cried in his arms as he tenderly soothed me. I cried for Mirabella and her unborn baby, and for Isaac and Tex, and Irish too. And I kept crying until my eyes were raw and my chest ached with exhaustion and grief.

When he was sure my tears had stopped, the tops of his fingers found my chin and lifted it. "You're safe. I promise. Because I will do everything in my power to keep you safe."

My chin quivered. Images of Mirabella's lifeless body in my arms were hard to shut out. "How?"

"Whoever is doing this is not some magical god. He's human. That means he is flawed. He'll make a mistake. And when he does, I'll be there to make him pay."

CHAPTER 24

CADE

"You need to take time off work," I said to Indy as she stood at the mirror brushing her hair. I watched as she pulled it back into a ponytail and secured it with a hair tie.

She raised her eyebrow at me.

"You're kidding me, right?"

"No." I moved to stand behind her and looked at her in the mirror. "We're in the middle of a lockdown."

"And I have a job. A job I've just started. I can't take time off."

"Then quit."

She reached for her jacket and pulled it on. "Yeah, that's not going to happen."

"I can't protect you at the hospital."

"Just as well the hospital is full of security." She sat on the end of her bed and pulled on her knee-high boots, leaning forward to zip them up. When she sat up she smiled at me and all I could think about was how beautiful she was. If anything happened to her . . . "I'll take an escort to and from the hospital. No one is going to get me while I'm at work. Lockdown or no lockdown, life has to go on."

She stood up and came to me, wrapping her arms around my neck. She smiled seductively as she reached up and brought her lips to mine. Her kiss was slow and teasing.

"I've got a couple of hours before my shift starts," she said, making me hard as she dragged her tongue along my jaw.

Christ, this woman was my weakness.

She was also a welcome distraction from the turmoil taking place inside.

I kissed her fiercely and crushed her to me. Making love to her was always a welcome relief from the seriousness of our situation. For a small patch in time, I could lose myself in the bliss of her touch and the magic of her body. I walked her backwards toward the bed, removing her jacket and unbuttoning her silk shirt. When her hand found the front of my jeans and began to rub over the hard ridge of my cock, a deep groan left me.

"You're not going to do what I ask you, are you?" I asked against her lips as we started to struggle out of our clothes.

"Not a chance," she replied.

Our mouths parted long enough for me to pull my t-shirt over my head and for Indy to remove her shirt. The sight of her full, creamy breasts encased in her lacy bra made me painfully hard, and when she removed it and let them spill free it sent me over the edge. I pulled her back to me and took one hard nipple into my mouth, sucking it with my lips and teasing it with my tongue. She moaned and pushed her hands through my hair, her breathing coming quick.

When my phone rang, I ignored it.

But when it started ringing again, I growled and reached for it.

It was the prospect. And he was on Jacob-watch, so I answered it.

"We've got a situation," he said. "Jacob discharged himself."

The prospect had been perched outside Jacob's room since he'd been admitted.

"Please tell me you've still got your eyes on him," I said, adjusting the front of my jeans.

"He stuck a gun in my face. Told me to fuck off or he'd shoot me between the fucking eyes. So, no. I don't have my eyes on him."

Fuck. We didn't want Jacob to be alone because we didn't know what he was capable of doing. "What happened?"

"He went to the funeral home. He was inside for about ten minutes and then came storming out." He paused and then added, "He was carrying a handbag."

"A handbag?" A sudden realization shot up my spine. *Mirabella's belongings.* "Okay, I'm on it."

I hung up. I had to get over to Jacob's house.

"What's wrong?" Indy asked, already buttoning up her silk shirt.

"Jacob. He discharged himself and visited the funeral home. He left with Mirabella's handbag."

"Oh, hell," Indy whispered. She put her arm on mine. "Her sonogram was in her handbag."

"Jesus Christ!" I grabbed my car keys off the dressing table. Jacob was going to find the sonogram, if he hadn't already, and lose his shit.

"I'm coming with you," Indy said.

I'd learned a while ago not to fight with Indy. I'd get there sooner if I didn't.

Twenty minutes later, we pulled into Jacob's driveway. The shades were drawn and the front door was closed. There was no answer when I knocked, but I could smell fresh cigarette smoke coming from inside the house. When I tried the door, it opened. Jacob was sitting in a chair in the living room, a fifth of Jack Daniel's resting between his legs. Without looking at us, he took a swig.

"Did you know?" His deep voice broke the stillness. He stared straight ahead, a cigarette burning between his fingers.

"Know what?" I asked.

He held up the piece of paper in his hand and looked at Indy.

"I found it in her handbag," he said.

I took the paper from him. It was the sonogram. Behind me, Indy exhaled deeply.

"Is it true?" Jacob asked, looking away as he took another swig from the liquor bottle. "Was she pregnant?"

Indy stepped forward. "Jacob, I'm so sorry—"

"Is it true?" He snapped.

Indy paused and then nodded. "Yes. She was pregnant."

Pain washed over Jacob's face. He closed his eyes as if to brace himself against the agony, his fingers gripping the arms of the chair.

"It says she was fourteen weeks. Does that mean she knew what the sex was?"

"Yes," Indy whispered. "She knew."

More life seemed to drain from his face.

"Was it my son or my daughter who was murdered with her?" he asked.

Indy glanced at me but then turned back to Jacob. My girl was strong. She could handle this. "It was a girl," she said calmly.

Jacob's eyes closed and his chin quivered with something close to torture and rage. He took another swig of whiskey and his façade finally cracked beneath the weight of his pain, and he broke down. I took the cigarette from him and smashed it out in the ashtray, then took him by the arm.

"Come on, brother, I'm taking you home."

He shook me off.

"I'm staying here!" he said sharply. And I could tell by the darkness in his eyes that he meant it. "I don't want to leave. I can smell her here. I can feel her." He collapsed back into the chair and his face crumpled again. "Out there she's gone. But in here, in our home, she's everywhere."

"Then I'm staying with you," I said.

He took another mouthful from the bottle. "I don't need a fucking babysitter."

"No, you don't. But I'm staying here to help you finish this bottle." I took it from him and drank down a mouthful. Whiskey burned its way down my throat and spread through my chest. I looked at Indy and she nodded.

"I'll come by tomorrow and pick you up," she said.

"No. Leave the car here. I'll get Vader and Maverick to pick you up and escort you to and from work." Indy wasn't going anywhere on her own. "And I want you to stay at the clubhouse tonight, okay?"

For a moment, she looked like she was going to protest, but she didn't. Instead, she nodded and then walked over to Jacob and crouched down.

"She had only just found out and was going to tell you that night. She wanted to call her Hope. Because it was what you had given her from the moment she'd met you. Hope."

Tears streamed down Jacob's face but he said nothing. There was nothing he could say.

There was nothing anyone could say.

CHAPTER 25

INDY

Mirabella was buried on a cloudless Fall morning in November. While Isaac's funeral had been somber and dramatic with a stormy sky, Mirabella was buried in the beautiful warmth of the Mississippi sunshine. Her closed coffin was draped in a sea of magnolias and irises, her favorite flowers, and in the center of the arrangement was a small envelope addressed to *Mirabella and Hope*. It was a final farewell from a grieving husband and father-to-be.

Jacob was inconsolable. It was like the light had gone out of him.

Finally sober for the first time since his wife's murder, he wasn't able to cope with his grief, and at one stage his knees crumpled beneath him and Cade and Caleb had to hold him up. He was devastated. Broken. *Destroyed*.

Afterwards, when everyone went to the wake at the clubhouse, Jacob sat motionless in his chair at her graveside, staring with unseeing eyes at her coffin as tears spilled down his cheeks.

Cade, Caleb, and I hung back. I was gutted. My chest full of grief. But it wasn't even in the realm of Jacob's pain.

Suddenly rising to his feet, Jacob walked toward his wife's coffin, his eyes dazed and unfocused, his face slack with despondence, his arms hanging motionless at his side. I linked my fingers into Cade's big hand and we glanced at one another, worried. Then, just as suddenly as he had stood up, Jacob dropped to his knees and fell backwards, his broad chest exposed to the sky as a primal roar ripped out of the very core of him to shatter the stillness of the afternoon.

Tears streamed down my face as I watched him unravel in front of us, his pain exposed, his body rigid and stiff with the anguish erupting from him. Veins bulged like ropes in his neck and forehead as his roar grew hoarse and rough, and the energy finally petered out. He fell forward onto all fours and hung his head low, his body wracked with the sobbing that consumed him.

Caleb and Cade went to him. Cade knelt down.

"Let us take care of you, brother," I heard him say.

Caleb and Cade got him into an awaiting car. He hadn't ridden his bike to the funeral. He hadn't ridden his bike since the day Mirabella had died, and it was probably a good thing because he was in no state to operate a vehicle. Cade opened the door for me and I slid into the backseat beside Jacob, curling my hand in his and holding it tight during the ride to the wake.

Mirabella's parents had organized the celebration of her life at Jacob and Mirabella's home, and the backyard was full of friends and family, drinking and celebrating the beautiful young woman we had all loved and cherished. Everywhere you looked there were flowers and photographs of a smiling Mirabella, and every time I glanced at her smiling face, I couldn't believe that she was gone.

Unable to handle the crowd, Jacob grabbed a full bottle of bourbon and walked back into the house, disappearing into his bedroom with a slam of the door. He had refused any medication for his grief. Now he was going to medicate with liquor.

"What do we do?" I asked Cade.

"We leave him to grieve the way he wants to," he said.

I spent the next hour talking with Mirabella's family and her sister Cora. I made small talk with strangers, had wine with Ronnie and my mom and some of the other old ladies, and helped to clear away plates of food from the picnic table when the sun began to sink and people started to disperse. As dusk turned to night, I went inside and walked straight into Cade, suddenly realizing I hadn't seen him for the last hour.

"Sorry, baby, I've been with Jacob," he said.

"Is he okay?"

He shook his head. "No. He is far from okay. Bull and Maverick have taken him back to the clubhouse. We don't want him to be alone."

He stepped closer to me and ran his big hands up my arms. He looked exhausted but still very physically powerful and strong. He bent his head and kissed me, pressing his lips to my ear.

"Let's get out of here. I need to hold you," he whispered roughly. "I need you in my arms."

I nodded and wrapped my arms around his thick waist, finding comfort in the gentle thump of his heartbeat. "Take me home," I murmured.

He bent his head and pressed a kiss to my forehead, then led me out the door.

CHAPTER 26

CADE

"You need to leave. You need to pack your bags and head back to Seattle."

It was two days after Mirabella's funeral and I was rattled. Watching Jacob bury his wife was like watching my worst nightmare.

Indy looked at me like I was crazy. "I'm not going anywhere."

But I ignored her. "You still have your apartment, right?"

"Yes, I own it. But I'm thinking of renting it out. Oh, and that's right... I'm not leaving."

"Indy, I'm not asking." I knew she wouldn't leave without a fight. But I was ready to make sure she would listen. It had been seven days since Mirabella's murder and we were no closer to finding her killer.

It meant we were all at risk.

Jacob was a mess. Inconsolable. His world had been ripped from under him and he was devastated. The other night, after the funeral, I'd found him lying in the dark on the bed he used to share with his wife. Conquered by grief. Clutching his dead wife's silk robe. His words disconnected. His voice eerily calm, yet flat and robotic. His Glock sitting on the nightstand next to him—the safety off.

We moved him into the clubhouse the next day.

"I'm telling you, you have to leave town until we sort out what the fuck is going on," I said. Christ. I would probably think about eating my gun, too, if I lost Indy. "It's not safe."

Indy climbed off the bed, wearing nothing but a tight tank and tiny panties. And despite my anxiety, despite my fear for her safety, the sight of her near nakedness still made my dick hard as a rock.

"I'm not leaving, and that's that." She looked up at me with those dark brown eyes and tenderly touched my cheek. "We're together now. And that means we're together through everything."

I tried to ignore how hard she was making me. This was serious and I wasn't going to let her sway me by giving me those big brown eyes. But she was my kryptonite. The one thing that could bring me to my knees and make me lose my mind.

"You could die, Indy. Do you get that? Someone is out to hurt The Kings. Three of us are already dead. Look at Mirabella. I don't want you to get caught in the crossfire."

She fixed me with fiercely determined eyes. "I'm not going anywhere. Do you hear me?" Then her expression softened and she reached for me by my belt buckle. "Now, will you please stop talking so much bullshit and come and fuck your woman?"

She pulled her tank over her head, revealing her perfect, naked body. Deliberately trying to distract me. "Or do you need a little more convincing?"

She ran her hand over the front of my jeans.

My dick didn't need much more convincing than that. I pulled her into me and kissed her hard.

"I don't want to hear any more talk about danger or me leaving, got it?" she whispered against my lips.

She pulled me down onto the bed and the move put me right at the beginning of where I wanted to be. With some minor adjustments, I pushed into her and instantly my mind went somewhere else. Her body. This girl. It was easy for me to get lost in her. And as I made love to her, the craziness of what was happening around us simply vanished and I lost myself in loving her, kissing her, bringing her to a climax, one, two, three times, until I couldn't take it anymore and I came inside her with a blinding wave of pleasure.

But as the warm glow of my orgasm faded away, the cold reality of the situation began to seep back in. Indy was my weakness. I couldn't be without her. If I left her, I knew I wouldn't be able to keep away. She would only need to look at me with those big, beautiful eyes of hers and I would go running back to her. She was my addiction. *My everything.* I needed her close but that put a huge target on her back. If someone was trying to take down The Kings—if someone wanted me dead—Indy could get hurt. And the thought of her getting hurt made me feel insane.

It was then I realized I was trapped. I couldn't leave. But I could sure as hell make sure she did.

I hated what I was going to do. And it was going to break my heart. But it needed to be done because it was the lesser of the two evils.

Either way, I was going to lose Indy.

But at least this way she would be safe.

I had wrestled with the idea for days, but had come back to the same conclusion every time. I had to get Indy as far away from this fucking club and this nightmare as possible. It would mean the end for us and she would never forgive me, but she would be alive. When I had second thoughts about it, I thought of Mirabella lying dead in Jacob's arms, her brains running out of the bullet wound to her head, and it was all I needed to convince me that this was a good idea.

Sandy was the perfect accomplice.

She flashed her wicked, bad-girl smile at me and closed the door to my room behind her. She was in a too-tight tank and the tiniest pair of denim shorts I'd ever seen.

"Are you ready, baby?" she asked, unbuttoning her shorts and climbing out of them. She was completely naked underneath.

I averted my eyes but nodded, my heart already dying a slow, torturous death in my chest. Indy would never forgive me. And I was counting on it. This would hurt her, but it would hurt her a lot less than a bullet to the head.

Slipping her tank top over her head, Sandy climbed onto the bed and kneeled in front of me, looking up at me with bright, come-fuck-me eyes.

"Well, what are you waiting for, honey?" she cooed.

I sighed and began removing my shirt.

No turning back now.

CHAPTER 27

INDY

At the end of my shift I was surprised to see Maverick waiting for me and not Cade.

"Cade asked me to pick you up. Said he's got some business back at the club house," he explained.

"You're not dropping me home?"

"He said to make sure I brought you straight to the clubhouse. Didn't want you alone at the house during lockdown."

I didn't know why, but a strange tingle took up in the base of my spine. Trying to ignore it, I climbed into the SUV, but by the time I arrived at the clubhouse, the tingle had morphed into a thousand startled butterflies churning in my stomach and my hands had started to shake. Something wasn't right.

Cade wasn't in the bar. And he wasn't in the kitchen or the meeting rooms either, so I made my way past the showcase corridor and headed toward his bedroom. The door was closed, which wasn't unusual, but as I stepped up to it, I felt an overpowering sense of foreboding wash over me. Shoving it aside, I pushed the door open and came to a stunned halt.

Seeing the honey-blonde sprawled naked on the bed was like electric shock therapy zipping through my brain. She was tangled amongst the sheets—sheets that were messed up by some seriously active lovemaking by the looks of them.

In that instant, my heart obliterated like confetti.

It was like all the air left the room and I couldn't breathe.

No.

Please, no.

The years peeled away, and suddenly I was eighteen years old again, walking into this very room, and finding the love of my life in bed with another woman.

But this time he wasn't in bed with her.

This time he was walking into the room from the small bathroom, fresh from the shower and securing a towel around his waist.

When he looked up and saw me, he paused. His beautiful mouth parted, but then closed again. He wasn't even going to try and deny it. And why would he? It was quite obvious what had happened in this room.

"*No.*" Was the only word my grief-soaked brain could form.

Cade didn't even offer me anything. He just stared at me, raising his arms slightly before letting them drop at his side.

A bomb of agony detonated inside of me, blowing me apart. A thousand broken promises rushed at me, the splinters twisting my insides into a tight coil until they burned with the pain of his betrayal and I could no longer breathe. I stormed toward him and slapped him so hard across the face his head whipped to the side and my hand stung. He didn't move. Didn't fight me. So, I slapped him again. And again he didn't move. His jaw tightened and flinched, and his teeth gritted with the pain. But still he said nothing.

"What?" I screamed at him. "You're just going to stand there and watch me break?"

I smashed my fist into his chest.

"Why? Why?" I cried. And I pounded him in the chest again. Asking him for a good reason. Asking him who he was. Because my broken heart was begging me to find out why he had done this to us. She needed a good reason so she could at least process it while she slowly pieced herself back together again.

But then my agony overwhelmed me and the cold ache in my throat made it impossible for me to speak anymore.

I couldn't stand it. I couldn't be in the same room as him and *her*. I didn't know how I was going to survive his betrayal, but I knew that surviving it started outside of this room. So I stepped back, tears streaming down my face, and stared at him. I wanted to sear his face into my memory, because when I walked away from him, it would be forever.

And then I fled.

Only then did he react. I felt the rush of energy behind me, heard him call my name as I ran through the corridors of the clubhouse, but I didn't stop, I kept running, blindly, until I ran straight into Caleb's broad chest.

"Hey, whoa!" he said, grabbing my arms. "What's wrong?"

"Let me go!" I screamed at him. And acting on instinct, I slammed my foot down on his boot so he would let me go because no one was going to stop me from fleeing the clubhouse.

"Hold up!" He came after me, but I didn't listen, I kept running, pushing through the doors and bursting into the afternoon sunlight.

I knew Cade's car would have the keys in it, so I ran straight to it and climbed in. Just as I'd thought, the keys were in the sun visor. They dropped into my hand and I shoved them into the ignition, and then gunned out of the MC compound, narrowly missing Cade and Caleb as they ran out of the clubhouse just in time to see me flee.

Out on the street, I didn't fare much different. After nearly running into a streetlight because I was blinded by my tears and crazed by my emotions, I pulled over. I needed to collect my thoughts. I had just committed assault and grand theft auto. But fuck it. I had just caught my lying, cheating husband in bed with another woman.

A tornado swirled in my mind and I couldn't stop my brain from rehashing walking in and seeing the gorgeous blonde in his bed. I gripped the steering wheel and squeezed my eyes shut with the pain. Random conversations and memories rushed at me. He had fought so hard for me. He had me in his every breath, in every beat of his heart, in every thought. Last night he had tenderly and lovingly made love to me, moaning into my neck about how much he loved me.

Seriously, it made no sense at all.

"I'm so in love with you."

He had pursued me with ferocious ambition only months ago when I'd came back for my father's funeral. He loved me like no man could ever love a woman unless he worshipped her with every beat of his heart. How could he just throw it away as easy as he did? I just didn't get it.

"I'm all yours. All of me. Forever."

He had really said that...

I played with the crown pendant around my neck. I was his queen. He was my king.

Why could he just throw it away?

He would have known I would catch him...leave him...

I looked up.

Fuck. Me.

My breathing evened out and I exhaled angrily. My hands squeezed tighter on the steering wheel until I was white-knuckled.

I'd been had.

CHAPTER 28

CADE

It took every ounce of my being to not react. My heart was already broken, but as I watched her burn with heartache in front of me, it broke all over again. I longed to take her in my arms, to kiss away her tears, to gather up her broken heart and piece it back together again. To tell her it wasn't true. To tell her that I loved her, and her only. That I didn't want or need another woman. *Ever.* But to keep her safe, I had to break my heart and then break hers.

But then she tore out of the clubhouse and away from the compound before I could stop her, and my plan began to unravel. It put her in harm's way, which was the very thing I was trying to protect her from. Without a security detail. Without me or the club to protect her. She was in danger. I shredded out of the compound on my bike. She hated me and didn't want me around her, but I had to make sure she was safe while she was leaving me. I didn't have to go far. A couple of streets away, she was pulled over on the side of the road and I could see her sitting in the driver's seat, her hands gripping the steering wheel, her eyes squeezed shut. I pulled up in front of her. She saw me and climbed out, and stormed up the sidewalk towards me, her face tight with fierce determination. When she reached me, she lunged at me shoved me in the chest.

"You didn't lay one hand on that girl!" she yelled. And then she shoved me in the chest again. *Hard.* "You asshole. You set me up!"

I didn't know if I should laugh or cry. The relief that ran through me was inebriating.

"Stop being an asshole!" she cried, shoving me again. "I know why you did it. You think you're protecting me. You're worried something is going to happen to me. So you make me believe you did something unforgivable so I will leave. I get it."

"Indy—"

"Stop!" Her hands fisted at her side. "This is *my* choice. Don't you get it? You're worried about me. But I'm just as worried about you. Stop treating me like I'm so damn fragile. I'm not delicate! I'm your queen. Let me stand next to my king."

"I need you to be safe," I said, desperately.

She shook her head. "You don't get to do that, Cade. You don't get to decide what I need and then act on it without my input."

I ran my hands up the length of her arms. "I need you to be safe. If anything happened to you—"

"Nothing is going to happen to me," she yelled.

I let her go. "You don't know that. I can't risk it. You need to go back to Seattle. Someone is out to destroy us, and until the club gets this thing figured out, we're all in danger."

"Then we're all in danger together, Cade. I'm not leaving." She looked me in the eye, her brown eyes fierce. "Tell me I'm wrong. Tell me you fucked her and I will leave."

I could lie.

I could tell her that I fucked Sandy. But in that moment, I knew it was a lost battle.

"I didn't touch her. But, Indy—"

"Shhhhh…" She stepped closer and placed a finger across my lips. Then she kissed me and my body weakened against the touch of her mouth on mine.

"Come back to the clubhouse," I breathed, holding her tightly against me.

She looked up at me, and slowly, she nodded.

CHAPTER 29

CADE

The plan was to get her to leave me. To get her as far away from here as possible. But fuck my plan. Fuck pushing her away. Fuck everything. When I thought she was gone for good, and knowing she hated me, it was torture.

Pure fucking torture.

So I locked the door and spent the day in bed with my girl. Holding her. Loving her. Making her come time and time again, because God knows I was so damn addicted to her I just couldn't stop making love to her.

When the pounding came on my door, the interruption couldn't have been more badly timed. Just as the taut tension in my belly uncoiled and released an explosive euphoria through my body and out of my cock, a violent pounding rattled on my bedroom door.

Waiting for the pleasure to recede, I growled and collapsed against Indy.

"Go away!" I barked.

But the door vibrated with another round of knocking.

"Get out here, brother," Caleb called from the other side of the wall.

Indy squirmed beneath me and grabbed the bed sheet to cover her nakedness. Reluctantly, I climbed off the bed and put on my boxers, opening the door and coming face to face with my brother's anguished face.

"What?"

"They've found a body out by the water tower." Caleb's eyes were dark, uneasy. "It might be Freebird."

I didn't need to say anything. Indy was coming with me if I liked it or not.

"Do you think it's Freebird?" she asked as we drove toward the water tower in her new SUV.

"There's a good chance. Buckman said the body had been there for a while, so identifying him by sight wasn't an option. But they could see it was an adult male with long, dark hair."

After Caleb told me about the discovery of the body, I rang Buckman. We paid money so we could make these types of phone calls. And because money passed over the table to the medical examiner's office in the guise of generous donations, it meant that when we turned up at the crime scene, Zachariah Sumstad wasn't going to turn us away. As long as we respected the rules of crime scene contamination, *of course.*

The Destiny water tower was on the edge of town, at the junction of two watermelon fields known as No Man's Land. For as far as the eye could see, the beautiful landscape stretched onwards, the dark green fields a stark contrast to the vibrant blue of the sky. It used to be a popular hangout for local teens, they'd come out here to climb the tower and drink their beers and smoke their joints. The view from the top was incredible. It swept past the Destiny borders and out toward the fringes of Humphrey. But after a girl fell to her death a few years earlier, the access via the stairs had been blocked.

When we arrived, Buckman greeted us. Over his shoulder, I saw forensic technicians dressed in dark blue jumpsuits crawling over the crime scene. It was a hot afternoon and the air was ripe, and it was obviously getting to Buckman because he had a handkerchief over his nose.

When Bull and Caleb pulled up, they joined us.

"Who found the body?" Bull asked.

"A county worker performing a monthly check of the water tower. Said he could smell it as soon as he stepped out of the van."

The smell was violent, and after a few minutes of shifting on her feet, Indy rushed away to throw up.

"Is it Freebird?" I asked, turning to watch Indy as I spoke.

"We won't know until the autopsy."

"Any visible signs of trauma?" I turned back to look at him.

"Sumstad said the head has suffered a lot of wildlife damage." Even with the handkerchief covering half his face, I could tell he was grimacing. "He thinks they were attracted to the blood and tissue."

"Any idea how long the body has been here?" Bull asked.

"It's only a preliminary guess," said Sumstad. He was climbing out of the ditch, walking toward us. "But judging by the rate of decomposition, I'd say he's been out here two weeks."

Irish had been dead two weeks.

"You think he came out here and committed suicide by jumping off the water tower?" Bull asked.

"It's certainly been made to look that way," Sumstad said.

"*Made* to look that way?" I glanced over at Indy. She was vomiting again.

"The placement of the body. The head trauma. It mirrors a fall. But he didn't throw himself off that tower. He was beaten to death."

"You sure?" Buckman asked.

"As serious as a heart attack, Sheriff." Sumstad glanced over at the body in the ditch. It was bloated and black. "This wasn't an accident or a suicide. It was homicide."

I walked over to where Indy was leaning up against the car.

"Are you okay, angel?" I asked, gently rubbing the small of her back.

She exhaled deeply but nodded. "I'm fine. It's just . . . hot."

I put my arm around her. "Come on, I'll take you home."

She paused. "Is it Freebird?"

I shook my head. "We don't know yet."

She opened her mouth to say something, but instead of saying anything, she rushed around to the side of the car and dry heaved.

"That's it, I'm getting you home."

"No, I'm fine." She glanced over at the remains in the ditch. "It's the smell. And the fact that we both know that it's Freebird lying over there."

I wrapped my arms around her and pulled her against my chest, my fingers caressing her shoulders.

She was right.

I had no doubt it was Freebird. He'd been beaten and left there to rot in the hot Mississippi sun.

Just like Irish, this wasn't suicide. It was murder.

I kissed the top of Indy's head and tried to fight of the real sense of panic knowing that Freebird wouldn't be the last to be taken out.

CHAPTER 30

INDY

The following morning I met up with Tex's widow, Dahlia, at the Miller Self-Storage facility just out of town. I had promised her that I would help her clear out Tex's storage shed. Thankfully, I was feeling better than I had been for the last few days. The long hours at work, combined with the long nights in bed with Cade, were taking their toll and I was prone to bouts of fatigue and nausea.

I took one of the club's communal pickup trucks so we could easily shift things to either Dahlia's home or the rubbish dump. Cade had appointed Tully and the prospect to tail me for the day, and even though I didn't like it, I understood and accepted the need for protection. It wasn't so bad—two big bikers would come in handy when it came to moving the big stuff out of the storage shed.

Tex was a hoarder and Dahlia couldn't stand it. That was why he had a storage shed. She hadn't wanted to clutter their home with all the things he wanted to keep. These included things like old bike parts, mementos from his youth like his old football jerseys and helmets, suitcases full of old clothes, and personal papers. He even had three big boxes of random jars.

I looked at Dahlia. "Jars?"

She chuckled. "Crazy fool loved collecting jars."

"Really?"

She nodded and threw the stack of magazines in her arms into the back of the pickup. Once beside me, she picked out a few of the jars in the box. "Coffee jars. Jelly jars. Odd, weird-ass-looking jars. You name it. He had a hard-on for jars." Her eyes filled with sadness. "He was a weirdo. But he was my weirdo."

My heart ached for her. Dahlia was strong. But she was hurting like crazy.

"Do you want to keep them?" I asked.

She thought for a moment and then dropped the jars back into the box. There was the sound of glass breaking, then, without a word, she picked up one of the boxes and threw it into the back of the pickup. She turned to me, squinting in the sun.

"Honey, if I'm to move forward without Tex, then I need to start over now. Ain't no point taking anymore baggage with me."

And with that, she walked back into the storage shed.

I threw the two other boxes of jars into the pickup and then set about opening a smaller box that was carefully stored under an old desk. Inside it was a bunch of photo albums and what looked like a scrapbook of some kind.

I knew Dahlia would want to keep the photographs. Or, at least, look through them first. So, I opened up the scrapbook and lost the next ten minutes in club history.

The scrapbook was old, dusty, its pages yellow, the photographs and old newspaper clippings all dog-eared and crinkled. There were clippings dating back thirty years, when Tex had first joined the club. There were articles about fundraising rides and charity barbecues, articles about the crack down on motorcycle clubs in the area during the reign of

Destiny's toughest mayor back in the '80s. There were wedding announcements, even one about my parents' marriage, and of course, several clippings about the West Destiny High School shooting.

But the article that really caught my eye was one I almost missed. It was snagged on some old photo glue on the plastic page cover and had folded over. I opened it gently so I didn't tear it and started to read.

"Girl Jumps To Death From Water Tower"

Destiny police are investigating the death of eighteen-year-old Talia Bennett who was found dead at the base of a water tower in the suburb of Clayton. It is believed, Talia slipped and fell from the tower in the early hours of this morning and was killed instantly. While there were no witnesses to the death, guests at a party at the nearby clubhouse of The Kings of Mayhem Motorcycle Club, say Talia had been drinking and socializing at the party before her death.

Police are continuing with their investigations.

There was a picture of Talia. She looked very young. Too young to be at an MC party, *drinking and socializing.*

I studied the photo for a moment. There was something familiar about her smile but I couldn't place it.

"Hey, Dahlia."

"Yeah, honey?"

I rose to my feet and took the scrapbook over to her. "Do you know anything about this?

She skimmed over the article but shook her head. "That must've been before me. Poor girl." She pointed at the date. "Tex and I didn't meet until the following year."

"And Tex never mentioned it?"

She thought for a moment, but then shook her head again. "If he did, I don't remember."

I nodded. "I've never heard anything about it either."

"Tex probably didn't know her or what happened."

I agreed. It wasn't odd for Tex to have kept that article, after all, it seemed he had kept everything club related that had appeared in the newspaper.

"Did you want to keep the scrapbook?" I asked.

"Give it to the club. Might be a nice thing to add to the showcase."

The showcase was where they displayed club memorabilia, like Hutch Calley's dust off helmet and dogtags, old cut styles, and an impressive display of historical club photos.

I tucked the scrapbook into the space behind the driver's seat of the truck, then set about helping Dahlia sort through the rest of Tex's stuff. It was a task that kept us busy right through to suppertime, and I was right, when it came to lugging old motorcycle parts and some of the heavier boxes, having two very big bikers close by came in handy.

But no matter how busy we were, no matter how distracted I got, there was no forgetting about the young girl who had died a sad and tragic death at the base of the water tower. And the sneaky suspicion that the Kings knew something about it.

Something niggled inside of me. Something I didn't understand. Something that told me I needed to find out what happened to the girl at the bottom of the water tower.

"Who was Talia Bennett?"

I had just walked into the house and found Cade shaving over the bathroom vanity.

He looked at me through the mirror on the wall, pausing as he searched his memory for the information. Then he shook his head and went back to shaving. "Who is who?"

"Talia Bennett." I opened the scrapbook to show him the old news clipping, and pointed to the grainy picture of Talia. "This girl here."

"Wow, what's this you've got?"

"It's a scrapbook Tex kept of all the news articles about the club."

"Cool. I wouldn't mind having a look at it."

"Are you avoiding the question?" I eyed him suspiciously.

But he simply gave me a dismissive look and casually went on shaving.

CHAPTER 31

CADE

Talia Bennett.

Jesus Christ.

I took a longer shower than usual, hoping to wash away the familiar guilt I'd felt when Indy had shown me the article. I'd acted nonchalant, avoided her questions and distracted her. But I knew Talia Bennett. And I knew what happened to her.

I didn't want to lie to Indy. And I wouldn't. But I wanted to think about what I was going to say and that meant remembering back to a really fucked-up time in my life. A time I didn't like revisiting because it was just after Indy had left me and I was seeking more and more comfort in the club. And drinking.

And women.

Twenty years old—young, dumb, and full of cum.

Like I said, it was a really fucked-up time in my life when my head wasn't screwed on right.

But Indy was waiting for me when I stepped out of the shower, sitting in the chair by my desk with her legs crossed and arms folded. She cocked her head to the side and raised her eyebrow. Her eyes rolled down my body, pausing at the towel around my hips, and then headed north again until they settled on mine.

"Put some clothes on, Cade. You and I need to talk."

Right to the end I was going to try and avoid the inevitable. "What's going on?"

"That is exactly what I am trying to work out." She gave me another raised eyebrow. "So how about you put on your clothes and then you can tell me who the fuck Talia Bennett is and why you're lying to me about knowing her."

Fuck.

"It was just over a year after you left," I started. "The club was having a party. I can't even remember what for. But it was huge. Talia was there. She was an MC groupie who had a thing for Isaac. I didn't pay her any attention. I saw her with Isaac a few times but didn't think anything of it. Isaac told me it wasn't serious. That they were just having fun."

"It says she was a student at West Destiny High," I said. "I don't remember ever seeing her."

"Apparently, she and her family moved to Destiny after we had graduated. So she was never at school with us."

"But she knew Isaac."

"He met her at the Greasy King where she worked after school flipping burgers or something."

The Greasy King was a popular burger joint between Destiny and Humphrey. It was a bit rough. Not the kind of place you wanted your eighteen-year-old daughter flipping burgers for coin.

"She got fixated on Isaac," I continued. "But he wasn't really into her. He banged her a few times but he wasn't interested in anything long term. So when I saw him drunk and kissing her, I confronted him about it. Asked him if he thought it was a good idea."

I cleared my throat. I remembered the night all too well. Alcohol had made me morose because the sting of losing Indy from my drunken, drug-fueled partying was still fresh in my mind.

"He told me it was one last bang for the road. Joked how good she was at giving head. I told him he was playing with fire, but he wouldn't listen. He told me to back off, and I figured he was right. I mean, who was I to go around giving advice about women? I had just lost mine because of my dick. So, why should he listen to me?" I sighed and shook my head, hating the memories seeping into my brain. "I was young and didn't trust my instincts. But I should have because something told me this wasn't going to end well."

"What happened?" Indy asked.

"It was really late. The party had wound down. Isaac and I were in the bar with Tex and Irish sucking back a few more beers and talking shit. Talia wandered out from God knows where, wearing nothing but her bra and panties. We were very drunk and high, and Isaac started going on about how good she was in bed, and how good she was at giving head—"

Indy sucked in a deep breath and closed her eyes. She knew where I was going with this story.

"I guess Isaac wanted to show off a little. So he encouraged her to show everyone. One by one."

"Oh, Christ, Cade." Indy pinched the bridge of her nose and shook her head. "Please tell me you didn't—"

"Not me," I added quickly. And it was the truth. "But the others, yes."

"Not you?"

"I told Isaac it wasn't a good idea. And I told Talia that she should just leave. Get in a cab and get as far away from the clubhouse as possible. But you know what she said? She looked me in the eye and said, 'I want to do this, Cade. After all, isn't that what a good old lady does?'"

I hated the memory. And I didn't get it. Why would any girl want an old man who shared her around?

"I told her, 'Isaac ain't taking an old lady anytime soon.' But she told me she was making sure he would make her his old lady. I told her I was calling her a cab."

The years peeled away and I was that twenty-year-old boy standing in front of a scantily clad Talia Bennett.

"You should go home, little girl."

"And unless you want me to suck your cock, Cade, you should go to bed."

"I can't make you leave, but if you stay, you'll be making a huge mistake."

It was the last thing I'd said to her.

"What happened?" Indy asked, bringing me back to the present.

"They didn't all just get their dicks sucked. They all fucked her. Isaac, Irish, Tex, too." I shook my head. "Or so Isaac told me later. I didn't hang around."

Indy's face went white. "Isaac, Irish, Tex . . ." Her eyes were widened with a sudden realization.

It took me a moment before it hit me like a freight train.

I'd been so concerned about telling Indy about the Talia Bennett story I had completely missed the connection.

First, Isaac had been murdered.

Then Tex.

And then Irish.

Was there a connection between their deaths and Talia's death almost ten years ago?

Or were we clutching at straws here and this was mere coincidence?

How did Mirabella fit into it?

And Freebird?

I looked at Indy, she had gone very still.

"How did Talia die?" she asked.

"I don't know. I woke up the next morning when the cops banged on the club door. Said a young girl had fallen from the water tower." I squashed down the memory of seeing the white sheet and the form of a body beneath it when we had ridden out to the watermelon fields. "There was some talk about it being a homicide, but they never got anyone for it."

"Do you think any of the guys had something to do with it?" Indy asked. She was frowning, but other than that, it was hard to gauge her reaction.

"I spoke to Isaac. He swore they had nothing to do with it. Said they'd partied and he had passed out on the sofa. Next thing he knew, the cops were banging on the door."

I can't make you leave, but if you stay, you'll be making a huge mistake.

"You need to speak to Jacob," Indy said. She picked up my cell off the nightstand and held it out to me. "And you need to call him now. Find out how Mirabella fits into all of this."

But before I could make the calls, my cell phone buzzed in my hand. It was Caleb.

"You need to get down to St. Gabriel's now," he said. "Jacob just went under a truck."

CHAPTER 32

INDY

The human body can endure great trauma— but not the trauma of falling under an eighteen-wheeler.

Jacob was pronounced dead on arrival at St. Gabriel's.

Using my staff access, I was able to get us into the ER where we spoke to the Head of Trauma, a highly-strung young buck by the name of Craig Malone.

"He can't be back here," Craig said, indicating to Cade.

"We've got a couple of questions about the fatal motorcycle versus a truck," I said. "He was one of Cade's friends."

"They could've been twins for all I care—like I said, he can't be back here."

I bit my tongue.

"Listen, I know it's not protocol having him back here, and I understand your attitude toward the MC because of who you think they are—"

"On the contrary, he and his buddies are great for business."

I decided to ignore him and adopted a more diplomatic approach. I placed a gentle hand on his arm.

"Please, I just need to know what happened."

He sighed, resigned to answering our questions. He looked at Cade and then back to me. "Paramedics spoke to eyewitnesses at the scene. Said he just laid his bike down and skidded into an oncoming truck."

I couldn't help but flinch.

"So this is a suicide?" I asked.

Craig didn't give it another thought. He picked up a file and started to walk away. "Don't see how it could be anything else."

He was right. It would be pretty hard to time that kind of assassination.

Maybe this time it really was suicide.

Or maybe—just maybe—the assassin was a lot better than we thought.

CHAPTER 33

CADE

Still in a state of shock over Jacob, Bull and I rode to Parchman Farm, the Mississippi State Penitentiary, to visit with Churchill. I was a little surprised he agreed to talk to us. But then again, prison could be a fucking boring place.

Churchill was a scary looking motherfucker. But it wasn't his size that was intimidating because he was relatively short and small, and I towered over him in height and width. And it wasn't the way he spoke which was intimidating, because he was quietly spoken and had an almost slow, sleepy cadence to his voice. It also wasn't the way he held himself, because his mannerisms were calm and still, almost unassuming and Zen-like.

No. What was scary about Churchill—the president of the Southern Sons MC—were his coal black eyes. They were cold. *Dead cold.* Like the empty stare of a great white shark.

When Bull and I sat on the other side of the glass from him, he fixed those demon eyes on us and I felt that look all the way through to my bones. *Chilling motherfucker.* Bull pulled off his dark glasses and it was like a damn stare-off between the freaky-eyed kids. Churchill with his satanic-black eyes, and Bull with his bright, otherworldly blue eyes. It was a silent throw down between the two presidents of rival motorcycle clubs to see who could out intimidate the other.

Me. I didn't have fucking time to worry about anything other than finding out if Churchill had any information about the attack on the Kings of Mayhem. And if I had to break down the glass between us and rip the information out of his throat, then I was prepared to do it.

"Let's cut to it," I said. "Who has the vendetta out on The Kings?"

Churchill's coal black eyes shifted to me. "Vendetta?"

"Four of our brothers and an old lady have been murdered," Bull said calmly. "We figured you might know something about that."

Churchill barely moved. He was sitting up straight, his shoulders back, his hands in his lap. He didn't exude the authority of a man with a big, powerful physique; he exuded the authority of a psychopath.

"Check your surroundings, gentlemen. I'm in prison." He slowly raised his arms at his side like a messiah. "How would I know?"

"Drop the bullshit, Churchill. You know any of us could run the planet from inside here," I said, glancing around the visitors' area of the medium-security prison. "I don't have time to do your little dance. So how about you just fucking give us the information and we'll consider it a gesture of good will from the Southern Sons to The Kings. How does that sound?"

A small smile curled on Churchill's small lips. "Cade Calley. Just as ballsy as your old man. I heard you're the new VP." His black eyes slid to Bull. "I'm impressed."

Bull didn't move as he spoke. "Yippee-ki-yay. Stop wasting my time. You have all the time in the world, I don't."

"Well, that is true, I guess." He looked unfazed. "But before we talk, how about you do me a favor."

Bull looked unimpressed.

"What's the favor?" I asked.

"I've had some privileges removed lately," he said, his eyes gleaming like polished obsidian. "Seems my cellmate came upon some trouble and cut himself . . . *shaving*." Meaning Churchill had cut him. He leaned closer to the glass. "He wouldn't stop talking. So I made him. But you didn't hear that from me."

My jaw tightened. Churchill was a menace.

No, he was a fucking psychopath.

"Get to the point," I said, my patience running out.

"One of your men is inside here."

He was talking about Zakk, one of our club brothers who was inside for assault. He'd caught his old lady in a compromising position with her boss, and in a fit of rage had beat him to a pulp.

"I'm not allowed *things*. But I have a list of items I would like. You can get those items to him and he can get them to me." Churchill smiled and it was snake-like. Slimy.

"Items?" Bull asked.

"Cigarettes. Tobacco. Chocolate. Condoms. Simple items."

"Condoms?" I raised an eyebrow.

"For trade, you see. They're popular in here."

Right.

"Fine, you'll have those items by the end of the day," Bull said. "Now cut to the chase, who has the vendetta with the Kings? Is it any of the rival clubs?"

Churchill smiled but it was cold.

"It's not anyone we know. Not the Southern Sons, or the Rebels. And it's not The Knights or the Tribe either. Behemoth and Saber put out feelers to their affiliates, too, but there is no vendetta in play. It might be better for you to think of this as *personal*. Not club related." He smiled. And again it was cold and reptilian. Then he stood up and stared down at us, his dead, shark eyes raising the hairs on my arms. "It's funny, really. Sometimes the very thing we should be afraid of is right in our own home."

And with that, he turned his back and walked away.

Bull stood up and put his glasses back on. "I'm calling chapel. Now."

CHAPTER 34

INDY

While Cade was visiting the prison, I was doing a little investigation of my own. I was on my break at work, lying on a hospital bed while a colleague rolled an ultrasound transponder around on my flat stomach. Her name was Lani and she was another emergency room doctor. A few years older than me, she had a kind and gentle nature about her, and a smile that was as calming as it was attractive. She was also someone I knew I could trust. She wasn't one for gossip or judgment.

In one of my hands was a pregnancy test I'd taken in the bathroom half an hour earlier.

It was positive.

And now Lani was doing an ultrasound to confirm it.

I let out a puff of air not believing just how poor the timing was. The last thing we needed was for me to be pregnant. Not with everything going on. And if Cade knew . . . he'd go stupid trying to protect me. I put an arm over my eyes to hide the tears brimming in them. I didn't want Lani to see them. I didn't want her to know what a mess this whole situation was.

"Now, just relax," she said, leaning forward and hitting some of the buttons on the ultrasound machine.

"Thanks for doing this," I said softly.

"I take it this wasn't planned?"

I shook my head.

"And I'm hazarding a guess that it's bad timing."

"Boy, you're good at this," I said.

She smiled. "Practice. I've seen that look a zillion times."

"That's depressing."

Lani's smile was warm as she looked at the screen of grey shadows in front of her.

"Listen, if we all waited for better timing, then it would never happen." She gave me an empathetic look. "I've seen that handsome man of yours. Seen the way he looks at you. The love in his eyes. I think those baby blues of his are going to sparkle even brighter when he finds out he is going to be a daddy."

Love flared through me when I thought about Cade and our baby, and the tears welling in my eyes finally spilled down my cheek.

Our baby.

I looked at Lani. "Am I pregnant?"

She winked and hit another button on the ultrasound machine, and suddenly the *whop whop whop* of my baby's heartbeat filled the little cubicle.

"That's a big yes," she said with a grin.

I felt both dazed and elated at the same time, mesmerized by the rhythmic thump filling my ears.

Our baby.

But then I thought of Mirabella and Jacob. And then Isaac, Freebird, Irish, and Tex, and my heart sank. This couldn't have come at a worst time. The club was under attack and Cade was distracted. He didn't need another thing to worry about.

"Here," Lani said, handing me a print-out of the sonogram. Again, my heart flip-flopped and my spirits lifted when I saw the image on the paper. Nestled deep inside me, a new life was beginning to take shape.

Lani winked at me and gave me a reassuring smile. "I have a feeling everything is going to be just perfect. You and that honey of yours are going to make wonderful parents."

I had no doubt Cade was going to be an incredible father.

But was now the right time to tell him?

I finished my shift three hours later and went home, mentally exhausted from the *should I* or *shouldn't I* question pushing and pulling against my brain.

Running a bubble bath, I stripped off and sank into the warm water, breathing in the heady scent of soap as I tried to still my mind from all the chaos taking place inside.

Tonight I would tell Cade about the baby.

I had made up my mind.

He needed to know.

CHAPTER 35

CADE

Bull called Chapel, and when he did, everyone was expected to attend, no matter how short the notice.

When everyone was settled, he filled them in on our meeting with Churchill and the assurance he gave us that it wasn't related to any of the clubs he and the Southern Sons were affiliated with. But he left out Churchill's warning about it being personal, because bringing it up would only lead to wild speculation. Distrust was already shimmering beneath the surface, and left to get out of hand, cracks would form within the ranks of the club and we could slowly break apart.

We couldn't afford for brother to turn against brother.

But I knew that once chapel was over, Bull would turn his investigation inwards, and he would start looking into every King and their family.

Toward the end of chapel, we discussed Jacob's funeral. Because of the FBI investigation surrounding Mirabella, Irish, and Isaac's deaths, his body hadn't been released. Mrs. Stephen's was making funeral arrangements in the meantime. Jacob had spent his childhood bouncing between foster homes and didn't have any other family, other than Mirabella and the club. With Mirabella gone, Mrs. Stephens was in charge of the arrangements. His coffin was already in Picasso's shop.

Just as Bull called an end to chapel, his phone rang, and when the tone and subject of the conversation became obvious to everyone in the room, we all paid close attention. Finally Bull closed his phone and grinned.

"That was Viper up in Kansas. Said he and Barney got some intel from an informant. Said they knew about some scumbag claiming to have killed a couple of Kings down south, including an old lady. They got an address and paid him a visit." Bull paused, and even though I couldn't see through the sunglasses, I was could tell he was looking at his brothers gathered around the table. "Asshole got himself all beat up, courtesy of Viper and the B-man. Ended up confessing to the whole thing. Isaac. Irish. Mirabella." He grinned and pounded his fist against the table. "Goddamn confessed to all of it."

The room rumbled as the gathered men banged on the table, stomped their feet and cheered. But despite the celebratory vibe in the air, Bull warned us to keep our heads.

"Let's not start pulling each others' dicks," he cautioned. "Until we know if this guy is legit, we're still in lockdown."

"What do you think, Bull? You think it sounds genuine?" Elias asked.

"Viper sounded confident. Said he knew details only the killer would know. But I won't be convinced until I look the asshole in the eyes and ask him myself." He turned to Elias, Cool Hand, and Grunt. "You three get an early night. We leave for Kansas first thing."

I clenched my fists. I didn't feel like celebrating. My lust for revenge was as strong as the day Isaac had died, and I wanted nothing more than to come face to face with the man who murdered him.

"I'll go," I said. My eyes remained firm on my clenched fists in front of me.

"You've got an old lady in lockdown," Bull said.

"She has the entire MC protecting her and a security detail that won't leave her side," I replied. And it was true. There would be no way in hell I'd leave if I didn't think she would be safe while I was gone. This development sounded genuine. Bull had said it himself, the scumbag knew things only the killer would know. I didn't want to fuck around. I wanted to make sure that our MC justice was delivered hard, fast, and lethally.

"Let him go, I'll make sure Indy is safe," Elias said. He turned to me and gave me a nod. "You go and do what you gotta do. Take care of business for Isaac."

I returned the nod. That was settled. I would leave for Kansas in the morning.

I wanted to unleash some family justice on the man responsible for Isaac's death.

And tomorrow I planned to do just that.

CHAPTER 36

INDY

I was still in the bathtub when Cade arrived home. I heard the rumble of his motorcycle, heard him talking to one of the guys from the security detail he had tailing me, then heard the pounding of his boots as he climbed the staircase to the second floor.

When he found me in the bathroom, he took one look at me in the bathtub and his eyebrow went up, a lascivious look heating his face as his eyes focused in on my naked, wet breasts. I watched with sudden arousal as he removed his cut and lifted the hem of his t-shirt, revealing a body that was pure man. He kicked off his boots and I watched, spellbound by the ripple and curve of his abdominal muscles as they flexed and deepened with every move he made.

"Does this mean you're joining me?" I asked, the muscles between my thighs clenching at the site of him undoing his belt buckle and pulling off his jeans.

He threw me a heated look. "In a big way, baby." He removed his boxer briefs, his semi-erect cock coming into view. Even at half-mast, it was impressive. And I watched with hungry eyes as it moved and dipped as he walked toward me.

Again, the muscles between my thighs throbbed and pulsed with a need to feel that delicious cock nestled deep inside.

Climbing in, he slopped water over the sides as he eased his big body into the soapy water. Using his phenomenal strength, he pulled me over to him until I was straddling his hips and my very ready pussy was pressed up against the hard ridge of his now fully erect cock. Without words, I took him in my hands, and spurred on by the moan that fell from his wet lips, guided him into me, moaning with the delectable feeling of being filled with so much man.

Our bath was luxuriously large, which was just as well, because my man was huge, and even with so much space, I still only had just enough room to fit my knees comfortably on either side of him as I rode him.

"Fuck, baby, you're so fucking beautiful," he said roughly, running his wet hands over my breasts. He was breathing hard and his brows were drawn in with pleasure as I slowly moved my hips over his, my pussy stroking and clenching around his cock.

I was driven on by the fierce masculinity of him and the idea that he had planted his baby inside me. I trailed my fingers down his powerful chest and over the bumps and grooves of his abdominals, making him flinch and clench beneath my touch. He smiled and it was devastating. White teeth. Dimples. I bent my head down and kissed him, drinking in his beautiful smile, my tongue plunging deep into his mouth, shamelessly desperate and needy to possess all of him. Slowly, I rocked against him, and my orgasm began to unfurl deep within my belly, and I moaned against his lips, pulling away to straighten. Using his shoulders for balance, I rode him faster, his gloriously hard cock hitting all the delicious nerves and building the hunger in me. My head fell back as my climax overpowered me and I cried out, my moans echoing around the bathroom as I pulsed and came all over Cade's cock.

I stilled, my body quaking above him as the last lingering sensations of my orgasm slowly eddied away.

"Damn, baby, you look amazing when you come," Cade rasped. I felt his pulse throb inside of me, and when my sensitivity eased and I could move against him without jolting and flinching, I slowly started to ride him again. I'd taken my orgasm, now I was going to watch him as I gave him his. I licked my lips and he watched my tongue slide across my mouth, his breathing coming quicker as I rolled my hips slowly over his, my pussy caressing him, my inner muscles clenching and releasing, stroking him, driving him toward the madness of coming. His big hands found my hips and took command of my thrusts. He groaned, his brows drawn in, his breath coming in pants as he continued to grind me back and forth over him. Powerful waves of pleasure rolled through me, sending me toppling over the edge again, and my second orgasm crashed into the crescendo of his first. We both cried out, our bodies working furiously together until the tension in us burst into flame and we came in unison.

I collapsed against him, utterly spent, and enjoyed the thunderous thumping of his heartbeat against my cheek. He reached up and guided my face to his, and kissed me tenderly, his lips moving leisurely over mine, his fingers pressing into my jaw as he held me to him.

When our breathing leveled and our heartbeats eased, I settled against him again and enjoyed the calmness and comfort of his tender fingers as they trailed up and down my bare back.

"I love you," I murmured. Then I thought of our baby and I smiled against his warm, naked chest.

"And I love you, angel," he replied, his deep and masculine voice echoing around the bathroom.

I sat up. It was time to let him know he was going to be a father. I moved and felt him leave my body as I eased across the bath to sit opposite him. The water had cooled, so I turned on the faucet until the water was warmer.

"I've got something to tell you," I said, the butterflies in my stomach taking flight.

"Me, too," he said. And I was momentarily distracted by him as he washed cum from his cock. It was still hard and impressive.

"What?" I asked, surprised.

His cock disappeared under a layer of soapy bubbles.

"I'm heading up to Kansas City tomorrow. We're leaving early in the morning."

"Kansas City?"

"A couple of Kings ran into a tweaker who bragged about killing a couple of Mississippi Kings and an old lady."

"You think it's genuine?"

He placed his hands over the rim of the bath and hauled his large body into a more upright position. "We're going to check it out. It could be. They said he knew a lot of the details. It's worth checking it out."

"And if it is?"

His face darkened. "Then I'm going to kill him."

I didn't tell him about the baby.

After hearing about his planned visit to Kansas City, the timing didn't seem right.

So I spent the night with him, silently holding my secret close to my chest, occasionally smiling to myself when I thought about the tiny life growing inside of me. When he got back from Kansas I would tell him.

After dinner, he took me to our bed and made love to me again with an exquisite tenderness. He moved slowly into me, his bulk blanketing me as his mouth and tongue devoured me. He made me tremble with sensation and cry out with pleasure, and somewhere in the back of my mind there was a whisper urging me to tell him about the baby.

But I didn't.

We fell asleep in one another's arms, naked and warm, but at eleven o'clock my phone rang, pulling us out of our restful sleep. It was the hospital. Two of the doctors rostered on to work had come down with a bad case of the flu and they needed me to go in.

"Let me drive you," Cade urged, his voice husky with sleep.

"I will call the security guys. They can follow me." I kissed him and he wrapped his arms around me. "Plus, you're leaving early. You need your sleep."

"I don't like you leaving so late," he said.

I kissed his jaw. "I'll have security with me the whole way."

He murmured. "I'll ring them. I want to make sure they see you inside the hospital. What time does your shift end?"

"They only need me until five."

While I showered and dressed, Cade organized the security detail.

"I've told them to make sure they collect you from inside the hospital when you finish," he said.

I crawled across his body to kiss him goodbye.

"Don't worry, baby. I'm perfectly safe."

CHAPTER 37

CADE

I was supposed to leave early but I wanted to see Indy before I left. I didn't know what was going to happen in Kansas City and I needed to know my queen was behind me in what I was about to do.

I arrived at the hospital a little before dawn. Laura, the cute little blonde receptionist, gave me a smile as I walked through the sliding doors, and when I gave her a nod and a smile, she got all coy on me.

"How you doin', Laura? Looks like a quiet night." I glanced around the near-empty waiting room. "You keeping busy with your crosswords?"

She held up the crossword from the paper and smiled sweetly. "Keeps me honest," she said with a shy smile.

I winked at her and her cheeks went a shade of pink.

"What are you doing here?" she asked. "I thought you'd be taking Indy to breakfast by now."

"That's exactly why I'm here, sweetheart. I'm going to take my girl for breakfast as soon as she's finished."

Laura looked confused. "She finished an hour or so ago. It's been quiet, so Dr. Burdett told her to clock out an hour early."

"Are you sure? Her car is still in the parking lot."

"Yeah, I'm sure. She said goodbye as she walked out those doors."

Alarm was a slow tingle at the base of my spine.

"Maybe you're mistaken, darlin'. Want to check with some of the other staff in the ER? Make sure she hasn't been called into an emergency or something?"

"Sure thing, Cade. But apart from a couple of split eyebrows from a college brawl, we haven't had an emergency come in for a few hours," she said as she picked up the phone.

As I waited for her to talk to someone still in the ER, something began to take hold of me. If Indy had finished an hour ago and her car was still in the parking lot, then something had happened to her and she was missing. When I'd phoned the security detail to let them know I was picking her up, they didn't say anything about her finishing early. As far as they knew, they were still due to pick her up at five.

Laura put the phone down. "Sorry, Cade, but Indy definitely clocked off just under an hour ago. No one has seen her since she left."

Fear stormed through me.

Indy was missing.

CHAPTER 38

INDY

I finished work early. It was a quiet night, and apart from a couple of kids with a few scrapes and scratches from a drunken brawl outside The Suds Bar, not much was going on in the ER.

I knew I should call Cade and the security detail. But it was just after four in the morning and I knew he had a long ride ahead of him, so I decided to surprise him by slipping into bed next to him and showing him just how much I was going to miss him while he was in Kansas.

It was a stupid mistake.

A stupid, stupid mistake.

Walking to my car, I was too caught up in other things to really notice what was going on around me. By the time I recognized the sweet pungency of chloroform, it was too late. Within seconds, I was plummeted into darkness.

When I came to, I was on a bed, my hands shackled to the headboard. I was blindfolded, but it was a little too high, so if I tipped my head back I could see a small sliver of my surroundings. I was in a room, a bedroom, perhaps, and it was still and dim, the only source of light was a small curtained window to my left.

That was when it hit me. I had been kidnapped and I was now a prisoner.

My instinct for survival kicked in and I began to struggle against the binds around my wrists. The bed shook and rattled against the wall as I twisted and jerked on the mattress, tugging on the ropes that held me prisoner. When that failed to work, I started to yell. I started to yell for my damn life. And that of my baby.

Almost immediately, the door burst open and a blurred shadow rushed toward the bed.

"Please, I'm pregnant . . ." I rasped.

"I don't give a fuck," came a growl.

I felt a male presence, felt his rage, felt the smash of his knuckles and the break of my nose before the darkness claimed me once again.

It could have been minutes later, it could have been hours, I had no idea what the time was, the only thing I knew was the numbed pain of a broken nose and two very puffy eyes. I was slumped against the pillows, my brain rattled and dazed from the earlier blow to my face. I licked my lips and felt the metallic tang of blood on my tongue. My mouth was dry and my throat sandpapery, and I realized as I struggled to swallow that the chloroform hadn't just burnt my lips, my kidnapper had used enough to burn my mouth and my throat. I needed water. I needed to get free before he killed me and my baby.

Panic tore through the haziness of my post-anesthetized brain and I pulled on the ropes again, suddenly terrified. Because if I didn't get free, I was most definitely going to die.

CHAPTER 39

CADE

I woke everyone up. Bull. Chance. Caleb. Hell, I was going to wake up the whole goddamn club because we needed to find Indy, and we needed to find her now. Because whoever was behind all this murdering bullshit was also responsible for wherever she was.

I was a mess and I knew it. And I couldn't afford to be. I had to keep my wits about me for Indy's sake.

I went down the hallway of the MC clubhouse pounding on the doors of my brothers, waking them up and hauling them out of bed. I rang my brother Chance, and then Caleb, and then I rang every other King on my phone, and I kept ringing until they all answered.

"You need to keep calm, son." Bull sat a shot of bourbon in front of me.

I looked at it and then slung it back. He was right. I was spiraling when I needed to keep calm and think straight. I needed to put the pieces together and work out who was responsible for this mess.

"The guy Viper and Barney were talking to . . . I want to talk to him."

"Already on it," Bull said sitting across from the chapel table. "Viper is chasing it up as we speak."

Grunt's hand found my shoulder. "You've got the power of the club behind you, Cade. We're going to get this asshole."

I poured another bourbon and slung it back. But the alcohol didn't calm me. The heat only fueled my slowly simmering rage. I gripped the empty shot glass. *When I find who did this, they will die.* Veins popped in my forearms and the shot glass shattered in my hand.

"Is everyone here?" Bull asked Grunt.

"Everyone except Cool Hand, Joker, and Elias," he replied, handing me a cloth to wrap around my hand. I probably needed stitches, but there was no time. And my panic far outweighed any pain I should be feeling.

Bull looked at his watch. "Cool Hand is probably five inches into heaven with his new Swedish girlfriend by now. Keep trying his cell. The fool's got to come sometime."

Grunt nodded and flipped open his phone.

"Elias said he was visiting some out-of-town pussy last night. He left just after chapel and said he'd be back later this morning. And Joker . . . he could sleep through an atomic bomb. Send the prospect around to pick him up."

Grunt grunted and disappeared.

I stared at the bloody cloth wrapped around my hand, panic tearing through me despite the two shots of bourbon. If Indy was hurt, or worse . . . I sucked in a deep, angry breath, my nostrils flaring as I forced the worst out of my head.

I wouldn't think it.

I wouldn't imagine a life without her because I would go insane.

I squeezed my bloody hand into a fist but felt nothing but the panic in my gut. I needed to speak to the informant who had told Viper and Barney about the lone biker who had bragged to him about the killings in Destiny

Bull's phone buzzed. No caller ID. Normally he wouldn't answer an unknown number, but in this instance he was ready to make an exception.

On the end of the line was the informant Viper and Barney had been talking to. Bull put him on speaker.

"Can you give me a name?" he asked.

"Ben. Beckett. Something like that. But it was probably some bullshit alias. This guy was a real tweaker."

"Can you give us a description?"

"I can do one better than that. I can give you pictures."

Apparently he had photos on his phone from the night he met the elusive biker.

"Send them to this number, right away."

"Already on their way."

Bull's phone pinged.

For a moment he studied the image on the screen, but then threw his phone down in disgust. "It tells us nothing. Fucking nothing."

I grabbed the phone off the table. The image was of a guy at a bar, grinning into the screen. The lighting was bad and Bull was right, it really showed us nothing. The guy in the picture may or may not have anything to do with any of this. We didn't know who he was, or if or how he was involved. We didn't even have a name.

I slid the phone across the table and sat down, shoving my head into my hands.

We were no closer to finding Indy.

Bull stood up and kicked a chair. "Fuck!"

But I didn't flinch. Instead, I lifted my head with a sudden realization.

"It's not him," I said, calmly.

Bull swung back. "What do you mean?"

I stood up. This wasn't about some tweaker up in Kansas. This was about revenge. Whoever was doing this wasn't about to get drunk and admit his crimes to anyone, let alone run his mouth off in a bar that was frequented by a chapter of the Kings of Mayhem. He was too calculating for that.

And I had a feeling it had something to do with the girl who fell off the water tower all those years ago.

Talia Bennett.

"I need to get something from home. I'll be back."

Bull tried to stop me. "You shouldn't be out there alone. I'll come with you."

"No." I headed for the door. "I'm probably the safest person in the club right now. He has Indy, so the last person he wants to cross paths with is me."

CHAPTER 40

INDY

I had blacked out again. I'm not sure when, or why. But when I woke up, morning light slid into the room via the small window on the far wall. My body was stiff and my wrists stung from the bindings. I was also dying to pee.

I tried calling out, but my throat was so dry I barely made a sound. As if on cue, the door to the room opened and I felt the same familiar male presence as before. I braced myself, waiting for another attack.

"I need to pee," I croaked, now fully aware of my aching bladder. "And if you don't want me making a mess of your sheets . . ."

He said nothing. He simply made sure my blindfold was secure before leaning down to undo my wrist binds.

I took the moment to try to work out who he was. Was that a familiar smell? Did I recognize it?

Yes, he smelled familiar.

"Get up," he said gruffly when I was free.

Not sure if he was going to hit me again, I cautiously sat up. My head spun with pain and the blood whirling in my ears, and I had to bite back my fear as I swung my legs over the side of the bed. Gingerly, I felt for the floor with my feet.

Where was I?

A pair of hands pulled me to my feet and then settled on my shoulders. With a shove, he pushed me across the room and through a doorway. Placing his hands back on my shoulders he hustled me along a corridor. I pushed my hands out in front of me, feeling in the air for anything I might walk into. My breathing was heavy and my pulse thumped wildly in my neck. *Keep calm. Keep calm. Take in your surroundings.* When my palms hit the doorframe in front of me, my captor shoved me again so I stumbled into the bathroom and fell.

When I climbed to my feet, he was right behind me.

"Don't try anything stupid," he whispered in my ear. I felt the unmistakable coolness of a blade against my throat. "Or I might have to get creative when I catch you."

The door closed and I took a moment to calm myself. When I was sure I was alone I quickly ripped off my blindfold. Light stung my eyes as I looked around me. I was dressed in nothing but my tank top and a pair of panties. My legs were cold and I was desperate for a drink, but I was more desperate to escape. I swung around, checking for a window to escape through, but the only window in the room was bolted closed.

Right. If escape wasn't an option, then I needed to arm myself. I scanned the room for anything I could use as a weapon. *Anything.* But the room was sparse. I went to the medicine cabinet, hoping for a razor blade, a pair of scissors—something! But apart from a cake of soap, a tube of antiseptic cream, and some kind of body balm, there was nothing.

I closed the mirrored cabinet door and felt suddenly overwhelmed by the situation. My head dropped to my hands. I had to find something to protect myself with because this might be the only chance I got. Who knew what hell waited for me when I left this room?

Lifting my head, I stared at my gaunt reflection in the tarnished mirrored door. The wound to my lip had been deep but it had scabbed over. Blood from the pounding I had taken to my nose had caked beneath my nostrils. Both my eyes were black and I was already showing signs of dehydration.

I turned on the faucet and bent down so I could hungrily gulp back mouthfuls of cool water until I was breathless. Straightening, I wiped the water from my chin and tried to steady my nerves. I lifted my eyes to look at myself in the mirror.

You have to get out of here.

You have to fight.

My gaze shifted to the dirty hand towel hanging by the basin and a plan quickly formed in my mind. Grabbing it, I wrapped it around my arm before I took aim at the mirrored door with my elbow. I had no idea if this would work, or if it would alert my capturer to the fact I was disobeying his *don't try anything stupid* demand. But I had to try.

I coincided a well-timed cough with smacking my elbow into the mirror. Pain shot up my arm to my jaw, and for a moment I saw stars, but my reward was the muffled crack of glass. Thankfully, it didn't shatter into pieces and simply cracked at the point of contact.

With fingers caked in dried blood, I loosened a shard out of the mirror and rolled it about in my hand, getting a feel for it. Granted, it wasn't a knife. Or a gun. But it could mean the difference between me surviving, or me dying.

Taking care of my need to pee, I considered my plan. As soon as my captor was close enough, I would stick the shard straight into his neck and run for my life. But I only had one chance, so I had to get it right. I would aim for the jugular and I wouldn't miss. It would be quick and it would be lethal.

When I finished peeing, I stood up and headed for the door.

I drew in a deep breath. I didn't know what waited for me on the other side, but whatever it was, I wasn't going down without a fight.

"Okay, you son of a bitch, let's do this," I whispered.

I opened the door slowly, inch by inch, holding my breath as I waited for it to be ripped open by my kidnapper. But as the second-story landing slowly came into view, I realized he wasn't there.

I was alone.

I stood there for a moment, barely able to breathe, barely able to control my pounding heart. My eyes scanned my surroundings. I was on the second floor landing of what used to be a family home. But there was something old, faded, and unloved about the place. Pictures were missing off the walls and everything seemed yellowed and dusty in the dim light. It seemed lonely.

This is a trap.

To the right of me, a stairway led down to the second level.

Probably straight to the front door.

I strained to listen, trying to work out if my kidnapper was nearby, but the house was still and quiet.

Careful not to make a noise, I crept along the landing, gripping the makeshift shiv firmly in my hand, ready to use it. Taking each step with caution, I slowly made my way down the stairs, my knees weak and my heart pounding like it would beat out of my chest at any given second. I was almost at the bottom of the stairs and the front door was in sight. Two more steps and I could make a break for it—for freedom. The front door was glass and I was more than game to crash through it if it was locked.

One step.

Two steps.

As soon as my feet slapped the tiles, I made a run for the door and reached for the handle.

That's when I heard him. His voice came from behind me.

"Nice of you to finally join me."

I spun around and felt my brain tilt. My knees weakened and I dropped the shard of glass in my hands.

"You," I breathed with disbelief.

CHAPTER 41

CADE

The scrapbook was sitting on the dresser in our bedroom. Forgotten during the craziness of the last few weeks. My suspicion that all of this had started because of Talia Bennett's death had returned. I could be wrong. The chances were farfetched. But I had to check it out and either eliminate it or pursue it.

I picked up the scrapbook. The top drawer where Indy kept her panties was slightly open, and when I glanced down to close it, something caught my eye. Tucked under a pair of white lace panties, the corner of it just visible, was a photo. I pulled it out and studied it. The image was grainy, all grey shadows, and in the corner it said, Baby Calley—9 weeks.

The realization hit me like a tsunami.

It was a sonogram.

Indy was pregnant.

The growl that erupted from somewhere deep inside me was as primal as it was fierce. In that one moment, I was insane with grief. Panic. Anger. Fear. It all collided inside of me, turning me feral with a need to do so many things. Find Indy. Protect her. Hold her and tell her I loved her for so many reasons, but also because she was having my baby. Then I wanted to kill the person who was behind all of this. Of all the pain and grief. All the agony. I would close my hand around their throat and watch their life drain away, my vengeance realized when their eyes stared into mine as their life ended.

I looked at the sonogram and images of a broken Jacob swung before my mind's eye. Of him on his knees in front of Mirabella's coffin, his head tilted back in agony as he cried for his dead, pregnant wife. My fear roared through me. But the warrior in me stood fierce against it. Whoever killed Mirabella had Indy, and I had to work out who it was.

I looked at the sonogram of my baby and felt a fierce protectiveness like I'd never known pulse in every beat of my heart. For a moment I was knocked on my ass by the thought. Indy hadn't said a thing to me about it, but I knew why. She wouldn't have wanted to distract me until my trip to Kansas was over, and the thought sent a rolling wave of guilt crashing through me. I looked at the date printed on the sonogram. It was from yesterday. Last night, when I had made love to my queen, she knew she was pregnant with my baby. But I was so focused on my quest for revenge, she didn't tell me.

Gently putting the sonogram into the breast pocket of my cut like it was a delicate treasure, I opened the scrapbook and flipped over the pages until I found the news article of Talia Bennett's death.

I studied the black and white image of a smiling Talia and the familiarity of her smile struck me. My skin prickled. I had seen a smile just like hers recently. *But where?* Frustrated, I peeled the newspaper article from the scrapbook and shoved it into my back pocket. As I rode back to the clubhouse, the question rolled around in my brain. Then Churchill's came back to me.

Sometimes the very thing we should be afraid of is in our own home.

That's when it clicked. That's when the pieces slowly started to move together.

"You took your sweet time," Bull said when I arrived back.

I didn't answer. I brushed past him, Caleb and Maverick and thundered through the clubhouse toward the long corridor where we had our showcase. Behind the glass was a ton of memorabilia of past and present club members. I scanned past the rows of scrapbooks, framed photographs, and the dog tags and cuts of the original seven who were now dead, until I came to a couple of photographs side by side. One was of a GI, his body rigid, his face severe with focus as he looked into the scope of his sniper rifle. Beside it was a smiling photo of the same GI. I held the photo up of Talia until their smiles were side by side.

They were the same.

CHAPTER 42

INDY

I couldn't believe my eyes.

The monster who had kidnapped me and kept me tied to a bed for a day wasn't a monster at all. He was a friend.

"Surprise."

Elias Knight sat in a chair with his arms folded, his legs parted, and a smug look on his face.

I felt dazed.

Elias. The mild-mannered biker whom I had grown so fond of.

My shoulders sagged.

"No . . . " I whispered.

His smug grin grew. "Afraid so, Indy."

I felt gutted.

"Why?" Momentarily my fight left me. I thought we were friends.

Elias looked perplexed, like he was genuinely surprised that I hadn't worked it all out yet. "You really haven't figured it out?"

I shook my head. "No."

I tried to swallow but my mouth was too dry and my throat too parched. Elias's eyes darkened as they focused on me and his grin slowly faded.

"She was my sister," he said with a dark edge to his voice. "My *twin* sister."

It took me a moment to realize what he was talking about, and with the realization came a rush of panic and confusion. "Talia?"

His brows dug in. "Yes, Talia."

My hungry, dehydrated brain struggled to process what was happening. I shook my head as if I could dislodge some of the fog. "So this was all about revenge?"

"Somebody had to make them pay for what they did," he said, his eyes hard and sharp.

I felt dazed. "But they didn't kill her."

"They might as well have."

"They were your brothers," I whispered. "You rode beside them for six years. *Six years*, Elias."

"What can I say, I'm patient," he said with a weird calm.

Again, I shook my head to try and clear the fog. "Why did you join the club that you blame for your sister's death?"

"Good question. Thank you for asking." He stood up and started pacing back and forth in front of me. "You see, at first, I wasn't out to kill anyone. I was going to simply break the club apart from the inside. Gain their trust, become a faithful confidante and use whatever intimate knowledge I had to unravel the MC inch by glorious inch. And my plan was beginning to work. A few ruined deals here and there, a few phone calls to the Knights or the feds. And I have to say, Indy, it was a *pleasure* to sit amongst them and feel their frustrations when their run of bad luck began. And to know that I was the cause of it all, well, that was truly poetic!" He grinned again, clearly pleased with himself. But it suddenly vanished and his eyes settled on me again. "But then your old man died, and man, I'd seen nothing like that outpouring of grief in my six years in the club. It was magnificent, and that funeral, hell yeah! That was some ostentatious bullshit right there!" The darkness in his eyes zeroed in on me and he stopped pacing again. "You think my sister got that when she died? You think she got a send off like that?"

Blood whirled in my ears and again I struggled to swallow "I don't know."

"Eight people. That's how many people came to her funeral. *Eight*. And not one of the men who stuck their dick in her showed up. Yet, when a dried-out, old, wife-beating drunk goes flatline, he fills up a church and draws chapters in from near and far." He shook his head. "That's when I figured, hey, nothing impacts these guys like a good old death in the club. And since I failed to get any real traction with the screwed-up business dealings, I thought to myself, hey, why not create more deaths in the club? And just like that, a new plan evolved in my head."

"You're insane," I breathed.

"No, I'm just fucking pissed." He brushed me off and looked away.

A sudden wave of weakness softened my limbs, and in the back of my mind I was vaguely aware of a dull pain heating up inside of me. *Period pain.* A new fear took up residence in my core. I needed to get to the hospital. I had to keep Elias distracted while I worked out a new escape plan.

"Caveman's accident—was that you?" I asked, trying to breathe away the pain in my womb and keep my focus on escaping.

Elias looked up and grinned. "Now, that was spur of the moment decision. I came across him and his two-bit skank by chance, and I just thought to myself, *why the fuck not*? Let's see how easy it is to do this. So, I rammed him. One sweet little tap with my pickup and they zipped off that road like a fucking pinball!"

He started to laugh out loud, almost maniacally, but then stopped when he realized I wasn't laughing along with his craziness.

"But Caveman wasn't involved with Talia's death," I said. The police and the MC had put it down to a one-off act of road rage. Not the start of a personal vendetta against the club.

He shrugged. "Like I said, it was spur of the moment. I didn't decide to start with those low-life thugs until *after* Caveman's accident."

He paused and bit his lower lip as he recalled what happened next. It was clear he felt proud of himself.

"Isaac's death, now that . . . that was some sweet, sweet revenge!" He drew in a deep breath as if the memory brought him much pleasure, and then exhaled slowly, savoring the satisfaction clouding his diseased mind. "That outpouring of grief and devastation was mind blowing. It was like the peak of a climax. The wane of an orgasm. I couldn't have imagined just how satisfying it was going be, not in my wildest dreams. I hoped it would devastate everyone, I mean, clearly. But I had no idea just how catastrophic it was going to be." He laughed again, that same crazed laugh of an unstable man, then sighed, disappointed that I didn't share his humor. "I have to admit, though, the others didn't feel nearly as satisfying as Isaac. But then again, nothing ever beats your first high, does it? Irish. Tex." He waved them off like they were afterthoughts. "Not nearly as exciting."

"What did you do to them?" I asked. I had to keep him talking. Stall him while I worked out my next move.

He grinned nefariously at me, and again looked pleased with himself.

"Irish was easy, stupid fool. He could never turn down a bourbon, so I got him drunk. Then once he was passed out—"

"—you shot him."

He clicked his fingers. "Just like that."

"And Tex?"

"I waited for him to get home, knocked him out and then placed him in the garage and turned on the car. Easy."

The police still thought it was an accidental death.

But it wasn't accidental. It was murder.

"Now, Freebird . . ."

My eyes darted to his. "Why hurt him when he wasn't involved with Talia?"

Elias shrugged. "Poor timing. He walked in on me setting up Irish's suicide so he had to go. He started yelling at me, calling me a murdering cunt as he rushed at me. So I grabbed the tire iron Irish had in his bedroom for protection and beat him to death."

Just like that.

My breath left me. Freebird had died because he was in the wrong place at the wrong time.

I remembered him lying in that ditch, all bloodied and broken, his body already starting to bloat. My heart twisted and I shook my head.

Elias waved it off. "Collateral damage, if you will."

"Is that what Mirabella was?"

He snickered. "I knew killing her would end Jacob. Slowly. He would die a painful, aching death without the woman he was so in love with." His eyes gleamed with a sinister brightness. "Just like Cade will."

Alarm flared in my chest.

I thought about Jacob kneeling in a pool of Mirabella's blood and wondered how Cade would cope with my death.

"But you killed Jacob anyway," I said, my voice shaky and hoarse.

"I had nothing to do with Jacob's motorcycle accident. That was all him." He shrugged. "Pity. I was enjoying watching him suffer."

Nausea bubbled up inside me when I remembered the rooftop conversation we'd had the night of Mirabella's death. How we'd shared a joint and he had asked me about the moment Mirabella had died. He wasn't asking as a grieving friend, it was a perverse question from a sick mind. He'd probably gotten off on it. Aroused by the devastation unfolding around him, psychopathic fuck.

I breathed out heavily, trying to calm my heart. He was crazy. An overwhelming sense of anger and grief washed over me.

"You think you've won," I said, unable to hide the disgust from my voice. "But you haven't."

"Oh, I know I haven't won. Because that would imply that I've finished, and I'm sorry, Indy, but I am far from finished."

Goosebumps spread across my skin. He was going to kill me.

"I'm pregnant," I reminded him.

He looked at me coldly, raising an eyebrow. "And like I said, I don't give a goddamn."

I struggled to swallow.

I had to stall him.

And pray that help was on its way.

CHAPTER 43

CADE

Elias.

He was the soldier in the photos.

I studied them again, his smiling picture against the photo of Talia, and my head scrambled to make sense of it all.

Was he related to Talia?

I wasn't sure what relevance this had to Indy's disappearance, but something inside me couldn't let it go.

Bull, Maverick, and Grunt joined me at the showcase.

"What's going on?" Bull asked.

"Where is Elias?" I asked.

"He was supposed to be dropping in on some old girlfriend but he hasn't been answering his phone. I told the prospect to swing by his place after dropping by Cool Hands."

My eyes darted to Bull. "How long ago did he leave?"

"An hour ago—what's Elias got to do with this?"

"I don't know. But I plan on finding out."

As if on cue, Bull's phone rang. It was the prospect. I watched as he answered it, my impatience growing.

"What is he saying?" I growled.

"He says there is no one home."

"Tell him to break in," I said.

Bull looked at me questioningly.

"Tell him to break the fuck in," I snapped. With my skin prickling with impatience, I took his phone from him. "Listen to me," I said to the prospect. "I need you to get inside the apartment. Because, if I'm right, then Elias has Indy inside."

When the prospect questioned me, I basically threatened to burn everything he owned if he didn't break the fuck into Elias's apartment.

Two minutes later, and with me still on the line, the prospect was inside Elias's apartment.

"Um, Cade . . . "

"What did you find?"

"That's the thing. I found nothing. This place is completely empty."

"What do you mean empty?"

"It's fucking empty. No furniture. No nothing. Whoever lived here has skipped out."

My roar was primal. My fear amplified. The one clue we had to where Indy might be and it was a dead end. Panic took off inside of me because I felt her getting farther and farther away.

Shoving his phone back into Bull's hand, I pulled my phone out from my jeans and found Davey's number. He answered on the third ring. He was the closest club member to Elias and I was counting on him knowing something.

"Wait. You think he has something to do with what's been going on in the club? The murders?" Davey asked.

The more I thought about it, the more I was convinced it was Elias.

"How soon can you get down here?"

"I'm already walking to my bike. I'll be there in ten."

He arrived in seven.

"There was this one place," he said. "I thought about it on the ride over here. Years ago we drove past it on our way out of town and he told me it was where he lived when he and his family first moved here."

"Do you think you can remember where it is?"

He frowned. "It was a while ago now—" He clicked his fingers as the memory renewed itself in his mind. "It was near No Man's land. Near the watermelon fields and water tower."

CHAPTER 44

INDY

"Why me?" I rasped.

Elias seemed surprised by the question.

"Because I've lost my buzz, Indy. I need the satisfaction of that first kill."

He was talking about Isaac's murder.

He paused and became very still, and his eyes took on a perverse glint as they settled on mine. "But I'm pretty sure seeing how devastated Cade will be about you will surpass it."

"Cade didn't do anything to her," I said, trying desperately to control my fear. I could barely breathe. "He tried to get her to go home. To leave before something happened to her. But she wouldn't go, Elias. She wouldn't leave."

"Well, common sense was not my sister's strongest suit," he agreed with a weird kind of calm. "Well, clearly it wasn't, because we wouldn't be here if it was, would we?"

"She had a choice," I breathed. I felt dizzy. I hadn't eaten or had much water in God knows how long, so I was dehydrated and fatigued. And in the murkiness of my exhaustion I was aware of a discomfort growing stronger in my womb.

"Yes, she had choice. But so did they, and they chose to take advantage of her."

"I know they did. But they didn't kill her, Elias. She decided to do that all on her own."

My words angered him, but he controlled himself. His eyes narrowed on me and his nostrils flared with barely contained rage. He was thinking and I was terrified.

"You need to sit," he said, suddenly snapping out of his thoughts. When I didn't move, he stomped over to me and shoved me towards a chair sitting up against the wall. He pushed me down and after picking it up off a small table near the front door, he thrust a diary into my hands.

"Turn to her last entry," he commanded.

I did as he told, passing over the pages of Talia's handwritten hopes and dreams, until I came to the final entry.

I looked up at Elias who urged me to start. "Now read."

I licked my lips and sniffed, tasting the familiar metallic tang of blood down the back of my throat. My eyes moved from the knife in his hands to the diary on my knees.

"I'm waiting," he sing-songed.

My heart was a wildling in my chest, beating fierce as my fear tore through me. I didn't want to read Talia's diary because I knew that whatever was on those pages would enrage Elias, and God only knew what he had planned for me then. But I had no choice.

"Dear diary," I began . . .

Tonight I died. Tonight Talia Bennett is no more. It all began when I went to the clubhouse and saw Isaac . . . my sweet, charming Isaac. My MC man. My lover. My addiction. As you know, we hooked up last weekend and he messaged me a couple of times during the week, asking me to come to the party at the clubhouse. I was excited because he had been more attentive to me lately, more responsive to my letters and phone calls, more open to my affection. That alone told me that his feelings were growing stronger for me, and if I played my cards right, and do the right thing and please him, then he'd see what a good old lady I would make, and he will make me his girl.

I loved him so much, diary.

So much.

But now my heart is broken and my grief is pouring into the open wound in my chest until I can't feel anything but pain. I can't say these words out loud, but I need to get them out of me so there is proof that this happened. So I won't ever let myself be fooled by love again.

The party was a big one. There were a couple of out-of-town chapters visiting, so the Kings went all out. A band. Loud music. Women. Liquor. Drugs.

Isaac was there looking handsome in his cut, his beautiful face angelic in the light of the bonfire. He saw me and I smiled, my heart bursting with happiness because that boy is just so fine he makes my insides quiver. But then he turned away from me, diary, deliberately ignoring me. He walked away and disappeared inside the clubhouse. I felt foolish because I had been waving to him and he turned his back on me and walked away. I looked around me and noticed a couple of snickering girls in tight skirts and tiny tops, leaning up against one of the barbecue tables. Damn skanks. Who were they to laugh at me?

I went looking for Isaac, I mean, maybe he didn't see me. After all, why would he ignore me when he had spent the week texting me to come? As I moved through the shadows and light of the party, I managed to convince myself that it was a misunderstanding, that he hadn't seen me on account of the shadows in the parking lot of the compound. Of course, he hadn't seen me.

I found him inside, laughing with his friends, drinking. We spoke but he was preoccupied. He gave me a drink, but then disappeared outside and I didn't see him again for a long while. By then he was drunk. Happy. And he seemed pleased to see me. He hooked his arm around my neck and planted a kiss on my head. I melted into him, feeling so much love for him, wanting him more than anything in the world.

Again, he gave me a drink and a few tokes on a joint. We sat on one of the couches in the clubhouse and we kissed. Then Irish, Jacob, and Tex joined us. We drank some more and we laughed a lot. They like me. They really like me. At one point, Isaac's big hand slid up my leg and found the edge of my panties. The gesture was shocking but exciting. He slid his fingers under the satin and found the slickness of me, making me gasp with pleasure as they slid into me. I looked around. Irish and Tex were watching with a wild gleam in their eyes, while Jacob seemed a little lost as he sipped from his beer bottle and focused on the swirling of his cigarette in the glass ashtray on the table.

At first, I wasn't sure. But Isaac's eyes were soft and tender as he leaned down and kissed me, his tongue stroking into my mouth as his fingers stroked deep into my body. I moaned against his lips at the glow of pleasure that grew between my thighs.

But I needed to use the restroom. "Let me pee," I whispered.

We were going to make love. And when he swept me up in his arms to take me to his room, I didn't want to break the spell with a stop to the restroom.

As I came back from the bathroom, I walked in on Cade talking to his club brothers, telling them to think twice about what was happening. When I walked in, he stood in front of me.

"You don't want to do this," he said. And it had made me so mad. Who the hell was he to tell me what I did or did not want to do? So, in an odd moment of defiance, I told him to go to bed if he didn't want his dick sucked. I don't know why I said it. I guess I was showing off, and when I saw how amused Isaac was, I raised my chin at Cade and walked back to where he sat with Irish, Jacob, and Tex. I climbed onto Isaac's lap and he wrapped his arms around me.

Cade looked at Isaac. "Don't be a fool, brother," he said. A drunk and stoned Isaac flipped him the bird and simply took a swig on his beer bottle. Cade gritted his teeth, and I can still see the tick of his jaw muscle as he approached Isaac. "She's jailbait. She has no business being here. You put her in a cab and send her on her way." Then he looked at Tex. Then at Jacob and Irish. He said, "She's someone's daughter." So I told him, "Do I need to remind you that I am eighteen and it is my choice to be here?" Feeling encouraged by Isaac's beautiful smile, I added, "Leave me alone, Cade. Go to bed." Isaac pushed his hand between my legs, his fingers creeping along my thigh and feeling for the edge of my panties. "You heard the lady, Cade. Go the fuck to bed."

Cade walked away with a shake of his head.

I stopped reading and looked up at Elias.

His eyes narrowed. "Keep reading."

Sadness welled inside of me and my voice was shaky as I continued to read.

> *Now I wish he had stood up to me and forced me out of that clubhouse—thrown me out or pushed me into a taxi—anything, except walk away and leave me there with those vultures."*

I struggled to speak. What did they do to her?

I remembered her earlier words: Tonight I died. Tonight Talia Bennett is no more.

> *As soon as Cade left, Isaac began kissing me. He whispered in my ear, "you sure you want to stay with me?"*
>
> *I nodded.*
>
> *"And with my boys?" he asked, his breath warm in my ear as his fingers found their way inside my panties.*
>
> *I looked at the other three Kings of Mayhem bikers. Irish and Jacob were handsome like Isaac. Well built, with big, muscular arms covered in tattoos and tight t-shirts over broad chests. While Tex was older, maybe by ten years, with a beard and longish hair. I didn't really find him attractive, but I wanted to make Isaac happy.*

When I nodded, I felt his lips curl into a smile against my jaw. "That's my girl."

The pride in his voice.

The smile in those beautiful eyes.

I would do anything for him.

Because I was his girl.

I stopped reading, but I didn't look up. I squeezed my eyes shut, and tried to block out the image of Talia trying to impress a disinterested Isaac.

"I don't want to read anymore," I whispered.

Unfortunately, it wasn't up to me.

"Read," Elias demanded.

I looked up and the tears in my eyes finally broke free and ran down my cheeks. Elias crouched down in front of me, his usually warm eyes were now cold and angry as he glared across at me.

"Don't make me tell you again," he warned.

I did as I was told and looked down at the diary in my hands. I ran a shaky finger across the page of handwritten words, my heart bleeding for Talia because of what she had endured. I exhaled deeply and began reading again, but my voice trembled as I tried to keep my fear at bay.

"It started with kissing. First Isaac. Then Irish. Then Jacob. When I climbed off Jacob's lap and onto Tex's, Isaac pulled his dick out and began stroking it. Irish did the same. But Jacob wasn't into it. He stood up and left the room, mumbling something about it not being his scene. But Tex was into it. He was really into it.

"Show them, baby," Isaac said. "Show them what you can do with your mouth."

So I did it, diary. For him. I took their dicks in my mouth and let them come on my tongue and down my throat. I let them stroke themselves to hardness again as they watched Isaac open and penetrate me. I let them fuck me, one in the mouth while another pounded into me from behind. I let three cocks violate and use me . . . for him. Isaac Calley. Just so he would see just how much I love him and how far I would go to please him.

And I felt like a Queen.

Sexy.

Fueled by their moans.

Their mumbled words and aroused groans like sweet nectar.

Because he would see. He would see how good I would be for him.

But when it was over, Isaac didn't take me to his bed. He didn't look at me with that familiar gleam of affection in his beautiful eyes. No. His beautiful smiling eyes no longer smiled. They were cold, disinterested ... empty. And when I wrapped my arms around his neck, he unwound them and pushed me away like I was nothing. He wanted a lady, he said, not a club skank who sucked cock for attention.

How could he not see that I had done it for him?

I begged him. Pleaded with him. But he had met someone else, he said.

That was the moment my heart stopped beating.

When my will to live ended.

Her name is Cherry.

She is away at college, but when she gets back he is going to make her his girl.

His girl!

The page was crumpled. Like it had been clutched in a moment of pain, and then smoothed out afterwards. Tiny creases spread like cobwebs across the paper. And I could see Talia, sobbing as she poured her heartbreak out onto those pages, and then scrunching it as the pain of her broken teenage heart overwhelmed her. As if she was going to rip it from her journal and screw it up.

> *So here I am. Broken. Used. My heart hurting like it has been squashed. I know what you are thinking—he told you he wasn't interested in anything right now. He was busy with the club. He didn't have the time to commit to a relationship. Yes. He told me those things. Told me he didn't have time. But he still messaged me. Still took me to his bed when I visited. Still made love to me. So I had believed I could change his mind. If he just gave me the chance, he would see that he wanted me as his old lady.*
>
> *Now I don't know how I am going to breathe after tonight because my pain is unbearable, and I can't imagine how I am going to go on knowing that he doesn't want me. I don't know what is worse, his cruelty, or the fact that I still love him after all he has done to me.*
>
> *I'm going to take a walk. I'm going to my water tower."*

I exhaled deeply. That was where Talia's story ended. A few hours later she was dead and broken at the bottom of the water tower.

I pressed my fingers to my swollen and burned lips. What Talia had endured was terrible, even with the words written on the page in front of me, I couldn't fathom what she had felt. And my heart ached for her. But it also ached for Isaac, Tex, Irish and Jacob, and it ached for Freebird who would never know about the incident that had contributed to his death. And for Mirabella. Beautiful, pure Mirabella.

My chin trembled and I fought back tears.

It was no excuse, but Isaac had been young—nineteen and stupid—and the boy Talia described in her diary was not the man he had grown up to be. He didn't deserve to die for his stupidity and acts of juvenile cruelty. Everyone involved had been young and stupid.

This was all such bullshit.

I looked at Elias.

If he thought I was going down without a fight, then he had another thing coming.

CHAPTER 45

CADE

"Think!" I snapped at Davey. "Is this even the goddamn road?"

We were in the Custom Chopper van driving on one of the sparse and lonely roads leading out to the watermelon fields. In the van were me, Davey, and Bull. And in the car following were Maverick, Caleb, and Grunt. The moment I realized Davey might have an idea of where Indy was, I wanted to climb on my bike and tear off after her. But Bull had stopped me. If Elias heard us coming he might panic and that could mean bad things for Indy.

Heavy, wooded areas fringed the pale dusty road we travelled down, and every now and again we would pass a firebreak in the trees and see a farmhouse or an old home, but none of them looked familiar to Davey. I was beginning to lose my mind.

He looked at me grimly. "I dunno, man. I just don't know."

Sometimes the thought that we were too late crept into my mind and it took all my mental strength to cast it aside. I would not give up on finding Indy alive. I'd lose my mind if I did.

The other thought was that we were walking into a trap. For that reason Bull had brought the others along. Elias was ex-military and it was more than likely he knew a thing or two about booby traps. Grunt was also ex-military and we were hoping he knew more.

Maverick and Caleb came along for the extra firepower if we needed it.

"There!" Davey pointed to an old billboard on the side of the road. It was faded, the image weathered and neglected by time, but you could just make out the smiling faces of two children eating watermelon pieces and the words declaring, *Juicy Watermelons Ahead. Visit Fassbender Farms.*

"I remember Elias pointing it out when we drove past. Said he and his sister used to sneak out at night and climb the billboard to smoke pot."

Hope flared in my chest. We were close. Davey was looking around him, and judging by the expression on his face, things were looking familiar.

I thought of my queen and I prayed she was still alive.

I'm coming for you, baby. Just hold on. Please, hold on.

CHAPTER 46

INDY

Elias rose to his feet and towered above me as he continued on with his craziness.

"You're probably feeling sorry for her right now," he said as he began to pace again. "But in the end, Talia got exactly what she had coming to her."

He stopped pacing and a look of disgust swept across his face.

"She was my twin. But she was a slut. Do you know why we moved to Destiny?" He looked at me and his eyes were bright with madness. "Because my slutty sister got herself in trouble back in Alabama. Messed around with a teacher at our high school. There were photos. An abortion. And it was a huge shit storm of bullshit, I'll tell you. So we moved to Georgia for a fresh start, and things were good until the story caught up with us again. The photos, they were circulated throughout the high school, and I'll tell you, Indy, kids can be assholes. They were cruel. Brutal. Not just to Talia, but to me, as well. We were socially ostracized. Bullied. And it got so bad that we had to up and move again to another town in another state. It didn't matter that I had met a girl who saw me for something other than the twin brother of Talia Bennett. It didn't matter that leaving her was like ripping my heart out of my chest. Nothing mattered but Talia, Talia, Talia!" He sucked in a deep breath to calm himself. "So we came to Destiny, and after a while it felt like we had finally found a place we could settle down. But then she had to go and ruin it again. After what she did ..." He ran a hand through his hair. "Everyone would know. It would be all through school and I would be forever known as the brother of the town bike. *Again*. Can you imagine what that that felt like to an eighteen-year-old boy? What it felt like when we had finally found a place where we could lay down some roots. The selfish little bitch. I couldn't let her ruin everything." Spit flecked his lips. Sweat formed on his temples and dribbled in rivulets down the side of his shiny face as his emotions got the better of him. "Why did she get to ruin everything because she couldn't control herself?"

"What did you do to her?" I asked.

"I saw her leave the house that night. Saw her flee in tears. So I went to her room. I knew she kept a diary, knew she wrote down all her stupid thoughts and feelings. She had left it sitting on her desk, so I opened it and started reading her last entry. Read all the things she let them do to her. Read all the things they did to my sister." His face twisted with disgust. "I knew it would be all over school come Monday morning. It was going to be Alabama and Georgia all over again."

"You went to the water tower?"

"Of course, I did."

When he confirmed it, I knew what was coming.

"I confronted her. Asked her what she'd done. She told me to go away, told me I didn't want to know what happened. But I already knew what she'd been up to in that cesspit of a clubhouse with those bikers. Knew what she had let them do to her. It was going to be hell for us again. People would look at us like the white trash we had been back in Alabama. Because of her. Because she couldn't keep her panties on."

"She was a young girl, Elias. She thought she was in love. Young girls, they make mistakes."

"She was a slut!" he yelled and looked at me like a man at the end of his emotional tether, his eyes wide, his face flushed. "She let them do things to her that no girl should ever let a man do to her."

". . . she made a mistake, Elias. She didn't deserve to die. She deserved your empathy, not your judgment."

He looked at me coldly.

"She let three men fuck her, *Indy*," he said my name with spite. "She let them defile her. Showed them what white trash she was." He stood up abruptly. "And who do you think would have paid for that *mistake*?"

Goosebumps rippled across my skin as I looked at him in disbelief.

"*You* pushed her off the water tower," I whispered.

His head jerked toward me. "Of course, I pushed her off the water tower! What else was I going to do? Let her live so she could keep doing this? Let her ruin my life . . . over and over and over again?"

"She didn't deserve to die!"

"She would have kept doing it, don't you see? Everywhere we went she would've dropped her panties for the next guy with a motorbike and a cut on his back. And I would've been the brother of the town whore, again and again." He was still for a moment. Then he straightened. "You know what I felt when I watched her go over the edge and plummet to the ground?"

When I looked away in disgust, he answered, "Relief. I felt an overwhelming sense of goddamn relief. It was finally over. I wasn't the brother of the town bike anymore. I was the brother of *the dead girl*." He gave me a pointed look. "And I'll tell you what, that gets you laid more times than being the brother of the town slut, that's for sure. Thank God for sympathy fucking!" He grinned like a madman. "Because God knows it got me laid a ridiculous amount of times."

"You're crazy," I breathed.

He laughed evilly. "No. I'm not crazy, Indy. Just fed up with her behavior and having to pack up and start over because my sister couldn't keep her legs closed."

His maniacal smile faded and he scoffed, shaking his head.

"It's ironic, really, seeing that we moved away anyway. My mama had difficulty getting over her death, so we moved back to Sweetwater, Alabama. Straight from one hellhole and right into another. You see, my mama got a boyfriend and he was brutal. Strong. Overpowering." Elias's eyes glazed over as he recalled the dark memories. He was still for a moment. Trapped in the past. The muscle in his jaw ticking as his mind took him back to the terrible times he had endured. "He did things to me that just ain't right. And you know what got me through the nights when he decided to brutalize me? While he was ramming his cock into me I would think about setting fire to that stinking mobile trailer we called a home with him inside it." He inhaled deeply to push the memories back. "And that's exactly what I did when he came home drunk one night and decided he wanted to rape me again. I was waiting. Anticipating his every move. So, I set that trailer ablaze with him passed out on the floor. And it felt so freeing. Making him pay. Making him die. The relief was a rush." He looked up, pleased with what he had done. "In that moment, I knew I had to make the Kings of Mayhem pay. I had to exact my revenge on everyone who had fucked up my life."

He turned away and began to flip the knife in his hand. Bile rose in my throat. His revelations were drawing to an end, meaning any minute now, he would try to kill me.

"They didn't fuck up your life," I said, delirious with fear and dehydration. Sweat trickled from my temple to my jaw. "You left town because she died. And she died because of you."

He swung back to me. "And I killed her because of *them*."

There was no point trying to rationalize with him. He was insane. His thoughts and motives were all twisted up into a giant knot in this brain.

"And now?" I was afraid to ask.

"Now?" Elias grinned evilly. "Now, I finish with you."

Fear tore up my spine.

"They will kill you."

"Oh, I don't doubt that they'll come after me." His eyes hit mine. "But by the time they find you, I'll be long gone."

"You're a fucking coward," I said as he walked toward me. The knife in his hand glinted in the morning light. "You say this is payback for what they did, yet you couldn't even confront them man to man. You crept about like a little church mouse only making your move when you knew no one was watching. You're not a man, you're a weakling."

Anger shimmered across his face, so I knew my words had stung his pride.

"I was going to make this painless. Quick. But now I think I might take my time with you."

My heart pounded in my chest. I had to make a break for it. If I could get to a window, I could dive out of it into the street and he was less likely to make a scene in public. It was the only chance I had left. So, I launched up from the chair and pushed past him, racing for the open window across the room.

I ran as fast as I could, but he tackled me and we both crashed to the ground. Pain shot through my womb and up my spine. As we struggled, he got me on my back and quickly overpowered me. He forced my legs open and pressed his pelvis into mine, reaching between us to undo his belt buckle. He was hard and I realized he'd probably been aroused the entire time.

"Now, I'm not a rapist by nature," he panted. "But when Cade finds you, I want him to know exactly what you went through."

He lowered his zipper and released his erection, and I quickly ramped up my struggle for freedom.

"No!" I yelled.

It's amazing the strength you can summon when you're fighting for your life. But even so, I was no match for Elias's power.

He went for my panties and I screamed at him, but that only seemed to excite him more.

"And I'd be lying if I said I wasn't looking forward to getting a taste of the tight little pussy that has Cade so fucking whipped." He tried to get his fingers into my panties but I was thrashing about too much. Again, this only seemed to fuel his amusement and excitement. "Yeah, I knew you'd be a screamer. You like it rough, baby. You better believe that's how you're going to get it."

His mouth went to the curve of my neck and his tongue slid along my throat to my ear.

"I'm going to enjoy this," he said hoarsely, his erection pressing into my thigh. "To think if Cade hadn't volunteered to go to Kansas in my place, I was just going to shoot you. Just like Mirabella. But him leaving gave me time. With you."

That was when I got one arm free and shoved my fingers into his left eye. And I didn't hold back, either. I dug them right in there and gouged it.

Elias growled and rolled off me, thrusting his palm up to his eye. I took advantage and scurried backwards, my mind frantically searching for a survival plan. Elias climbed to his feet, unsteadily, and I shakily rose to mine. Not wasting a moment longer, I closed the space between us and slammed my knee into his groin. With a cry, he fell to his knees, his exposed erection going limp from the pain in his balls.

"You goddamn fucking bitch!" he roared.

And because he was a murdering, raping, sonofabitch, while he nursed his aching balls, I kicked him in the jaw, dropping his murderous ass to the floor.

Unfortunately, I didn't have the energy for any more, and I began to see stars. And despite the adrenaline powering through my veins, I felt woozy and stumbled on my feet. I slumped against the wall.

No, no, no, no.

I was going to pass out. Elias rose to his knees.

But it was okay. Because right in that moment, Cade burst in the room with his gun firmly aimed at Elias.

CHAPTER 47

CADE

Nothing could prepare me for what I was going to see when I kicked in the front door of the non-descript, suburban home.

But seeing Elias on his knees, nursing his balls and a half-naked Indy slumped against the wall, made me see red.

Blood fucking red.

What the fuck had Elias done to my queen?

I raised my gun, ready to put a bullet in him. Hell, I was ready to unload the entire fucking clip into his head, but Indy's voice stopped me.

"Cade, no!" she cried out, hoarsely. She was conscious but only just. Her head lolled against the wall as she looked at me. "Don't kill him."

But the murderous rage pounding through me was hard to drown out. I had to calm it down, and the only way was to make Elias feel all the pain and suffering of the people he had hurt. Isaac. Tex. Irish. Freebird. Mirabella. *Indy*. He had to pay for what he had done to them.

"You murdering sonofabitch," I seethed, crossing the room to stand over him.

"If you kill him, you'll be giving him what he wants," Indy pleaded.

Elias smirked through the delirium of pain. "I've already gotten what I want. Making the Kings pay." He laughed, dazed, blood spilling down his chin from his bloodied mouth. "Gutting the club like a pig. Taking you out . . . one by one."

My rage was blinding and I was only vaguely aware of Bull, Maverick, and Davey bursting into the room.

I pressed the barrel of my gun against Elias's forehead.

Again, Indy begged. "Don't do this, Cade."

Elias looked up at me, his face already swollen from my foot to his face. Blood stained his teeth. "If you hadn't turned up, Cade, I was going to mess her up. Fuck her in every hole—" He was almost laughing.

"Don't listen to him, baby! He wants you to kill him. It will be his ultimate revenge. You'll go to prison. It will ruin your life."

"She's right, son," Bull said. Out of the corner of my eye I could see he was with Indy. She was safe.

But Isaac, Tex, Irish, Freebird, and Mirabella were all dead.

Jacob, too.

I fidgeted the gun against his forehead. "No court in the world will convict a man of murder—for killing the man he caught raping his girl." My finger was a breath away from pulling the trigger, and it was only Indy's voice standing between me and pulling it. I couldn't stand the thought of what he had done to her. To my family and friends.

"He didn't rape me, baby. Please don't do this. It's what he wants. Think about it, he doesn't want to go to prison. It will be hell for him."

I thought of Isaac lying dead in the stainless steel drawer. I thought of Irish with his brains splattered all over the wall behind him. I thought of Freebird lying bloated and black in a ditch, and of Jacob desperately trying to put Mirabella's head back together as she lay dead in his arms. My finger itched on the trigger.

"But he'll be alive. And as long as he's alive, he has more than what Isaac has."

Elias looked up at me, a hint of a smile on his face, blood dripping from his lips. "That's right, Cade. Pull the trigger. Pull the trigger, or I swear, one day, I will find your girl and I will spoil her—"

"Cade—!" Indy cried.

"I will fuck her. Eat her pussy—"

That was all I needed.

My index finger tightened around the trigger, and this time I didn't hesitate.

"Eat this, motherfucker—"

And I shot him.

Elias dropped to his knees, a red stain spreading across his chest from the bullet hole in his body.

"You fuck!" he growled, clutching his chest as he fell onto his back.

I loomed over him, pleased he was still conscious so he could still see me pointing my gun at his heart.

"This is from Isaac. He says *fuck you*."

And I shot him again.

CHAPTER 48

CADE

The wait to find out if the baby was going to be okay was long and tortuous. Feelings of relief mingled with panic. Indy was going to be okay, but there was real concern surrounding the baby.

Feeling helpless, I rode with her in the back of the ambulance, holding her hand tightly as she slipped in and out of consciousness, promising her that I would never let anything happen to her again.

In my head, I silently begged my baby to live. I put my hand on Indy's stomach and willed our baby to stay, promising him that I would be the best damn father there was if he would just hang around and give me the chance. He would be loved fiercely, I promised. Because I knew it was my son growing inside of my wife. I knew with the instinct of a father who so desperately wanted his baby to be born.

"When did you know?" Indy's hoarse voice broke into my prayers.

I looked up and saw she was awake, her sleepy eyes focused on me.

"About the baby?"

She nodded, and I could see a tear pooling in the corner of her eye. When she blinked, it dragged slowly down her cheek.

"I found the sonogram," I said.

A second tear followed the first.

"I was going to tell you when you got back from Kansas City." Her face screwed up and she pulled her knees to her chest, moaning in pain. She reached down and her fingers disappeared beneath the blanket. When they reappeared they were soaked in blood.

Fear and pain spun like a tornado inside of me.

"It could be spotting," Indy said to me. She looked at the EMT sitting next to her for reassurance.

"It could be," the EMT replied with a nod.

But I was a fucking rock star at reading people, and I could see the EMT didn't think it was spotting. Fear drove a stake right into my heart. Indy was losing the baby.

"I'm so sorry, angel," I said, resisting the urge to kiss her face. She was burned and bruised, and the split in her lip had started to bleed again. Christ, I felt so damn guilty about what happened to her. And if our baby died because of it—

"Oh, God," Indy moaned again and squeezed her eyes shut as another spasm of pain took hold of her.

"Can't you do something?" I growled at the EMT.

"We've given her what we can," he said, calmly checking her vitals. "We'll be at the hospital soon."

Indy squeezed my hand. "It's going to be okay, baby," she rasped.

I gave her the most confident smile I could muster. "Of course, it is," I said. I gave her a wink, even though it felt like my world was about collapse in on itself again. "Our boy is a mix of you and me. He's strong. He'll make it through this."

"What if he is a she?" Indy smiled weakly.

I ran my thumb across her cheek. "Then my heart is a goner."

EPILOGUE

INDY

Two days later, when I was due to be released from the hospital, Cade turned up with a bunch of flowers. He'd barely left my side since I was admitted, only going home when visiting hours were over and the nurses threw him out.

"Hey, beautiful," he said, leaning down and kissing the top of my head. He didn't kiss me on the mouth because my lips were still plump with bruises and cuts.

"Liar," I joked. "I've seen my reflection."

My face was a mess. Two black eyes, one broken nose. Cuts. Bruises. Burns.

Cade's brow furrowed. "Baby, I'm so sorry this happened to you."

Over the last two days, Cade had bounced between rage, grief, and remorse. When he found out I was missing, he'd gone insane. He'd felt overwhelmed at the thought of losing me. And then, when he'd found out the about the baby, he was terrified about losing the both of us.

"Stop apologizing. You saved my life."

"I should have killed him," he said darkly, and from the corner of my eye I could see the twitch of his fingers as they fisted at his side.

We'd had this conversation a few times over the last two days. Cade wrestled with not killing Elias. And I knew the only reason he didn't was because of me. He had deliberately aimed away from his heart. The two shots were meant to inflict pain. Not death.

I reached for his hand. "I didn't want that."

"But if he gets out of prison like Travis—"

"He killed seven people and kidnapped an eighth. Elias Knight is going to prison for the rest of his life."

He looked away and nodded, and I could see the burden of guilt on his shoulders as he thought about the last month. He blamed himself for everything that had happened—Isaac, Tex, Irish, Mirabella, Freebird, me, even Talia.

But most of all, he blamed himself for putting me right in the middle of Elias's crosshairs.

"If I hadn't been so blinded by revenge, I wouldn't have volunteered to go to Kansas. He would have to have gone and he wouldn't have had the chance to abduct you."

"If you hadn't volunteered to go, he would have killed me. He told me that. If he had to leave, he was going to kill me before he left. But you volunteered to go, instead. That gave him the idea of toying with me, instead of assassinating me on the spot like Mirabella." I squeezed his hand. "You saved my life, Cade."

I wasn't used to Cade looking anything but strong and confident. But when we talked about my abduction at the hands of Elias, he looked tortured.

I smiled up at him. "Everything is okay now." I smoothed my hand over my flat belly and felt the warm glow of love in my heart when I thought of what the future held for us. The bleeding had stopped, and my doctor assured me the pregnancy was out of danger. Cade and I were going to be parents, and when I thought about it, my heart overflowed with the love I felt for him and our baby.

For a moment, Cade didn't say anything. His brows were drawn in and he seemed momentarily lost in his thoughts.

"I'm done," he finally said.

I looked at him, confused. "What are you talking about?"

"With the club." He glanced around us. "All of it."

"You want to leave the MC?" I asked, taken aback.

He looked at me, the bright blue of his eyes sharpened with determination. "I'll patch out and we can move. California, maybe. We'll buy a farm, hell, we'll grow grapes and make wine. I don't give a fuck." He ran his hands down my arms. "What matters is that we're together—you, me, and Bomb." Cade had nicknamed our baby, *Bomb*. Because when he'd found out I was pregnant, it was like a bomb going off inside of him, amplifying his already fierce need to find me.

"I know you never wanted this life," he said. "And I've been a selfish fuck making you live it. But I'm done, Indy. We'll do it your way. We'll get out of here, start a new life, raise Bomb and get down to making more babies."

"And wine, by the sounds of it."

"Whatever you want, I'll break my back giving it to you."

He was serious. But I shook my head.

"Baby, you couldn't last five minutes out of reach of the Mississippi." I tugged at his hand and smiled up at him gently. "That's not what you want. And it's not what I want, either."

He looked surprised. "It's not?"

"No. I left it behind once before, and when I came back, I realized just how much the MC ran through my veins. They're our family. We belong here." I rubbed my hands over my belly. "Plus, I don't want this one missing out on all those uncles and aunts."

Cade grinned and leaned down to kiss me. For the first time in days, he cradled my face between his big hands and pressed his lips to mine, exhaling deeply as his tongue entered my mouth. The sting of my cut lip made me wince and he pulled back.

"I'm sorry," he whispered, dropping his forehead to mine.

I smiled up at him. "Will you stop apologizing and kiss me again?"

Cade's eyes sparkled down at me as he bent his head and did just that.

THE END

Next in the Series
Biker Baby: Kings of Mayhem MC Series Book 3

BIKER BABY
Kings of Mayhem Book Three

Prologue

HONEY

I was about to make a huge mistake.

And when I say huge, I mean, approximately ten inches' worth of mistake.

But after the week I'd had, it was just what I needed. A night of big bad mistakes with a big bad cock.

I focused on the mouth moving sensually over mine. The way this guy kissed had me pulsing in places I hadn't pulsed in months.

"What's your name again?" The guy with the tattoos and all those muscles asked between kisses.

"Let's just keep that to ourselves," I said, drawing his mouth to mine again and kissing him hard. "It adds to the mystery, don't you think?"

We tumbled through the door to the motel room we had just paid for. The guy behind the counter had hardly batted an eye at us when he took down our details. And I shouldn't be surprised. This place probably rented rooms by the hour.

We fell into the room, and the man who was kissing me into nirvana kicked the door closed behind us and pressed me up against the wall.

He pulled away briefly and his eyes rolled over me, they were full of heat. "You're so fucking hot."

I grinned and tugged at his belt buckle. "You're not so bad yourself."

When my hand brushed over the hardness punching against his zipper, I gasped. My hand went in for a second look. *Holy hell.* This guy was packing a giant erection.

An unfamiliar thrill ran through me.

This guy was something else. He had muscles for miles and the type of height that commanded everyone's attention.

I dropped to my knees and peeled down his jeans to reveal the biggest cock I'd ever seen in my life. I looked up at him, unsure how I was going to fit all of him into my mouth. He grinned down at me but it faded into a look of pure molten heat as I took him in my hand and ran my tongue along the length of him and across the shiny, throbbing head. My mouth closed over him and my tongue tortured the wide crest, licking at it, sucking it, curling and swirling around the sensitive skin at the base of the head. He groaned and it was primal. Virile. *Pure man*. His hands tangled in my hair and his knees weakened. As his arousal started to peak his cock began to dip and lift against my lips.

One big arm guided me to my feet and he cupped my face in his hands. "When I come, I'm going to come inside you."

He pulled my face to his, and with a groan, kissed me hard. He moved me across to the bed where he peeled every item of clothing from my body, savoring the experience by removing them slowly and kissing every area of exposed flesh. My head spun and my body clenched with every purposeful lick and touch of his lips against my skin. He lay me down and crawled over me, his hard body covering me in heat and rock-hard muscle. I'm not sure when he took his jeans off, I was too lost in sensation, too lost in the feel of his tongue on my skin and the deep moans of appreciation escaping him as he slowly worked my body into a fever.

I was drowning in desire when he reached for the condom in his wallet. And I could barely breathe as he ripped the foil package open and rolled the sheath of latex over his very hard, very big cock.

He crawled back over me, and the heat on his face and the vibrant need in his eyes made me forget to breathe. With one long, hard push he was inside me, and the sudden intrusion sent fireworks zip-zapping through me. His size opened me, stretched me, and he thrust into me with a physical prowess I'd never known, hitting every delicious spot inside of me. He was a lot of man to take. He was big, with broad shoulders and huge biceps, and just the sensation of all that muscle on top of me was enough to send pleasure soaring throughout my body. What he did with his mouth, his tongue, his body, it sent me crazy.

My orgasm was swift, its ferocity overwhelming me completely. My eyes closed and I clutched his massive shoulders as I cried out again and again, utterly lost in ecstasy. He thrust my arms above my head, grinding hard into me to draw out the pleasure spiraling out from where our bodies connected.

"That was amazing," I gasped, floating on the dizzying heights of my afterglow.

He smiled against my lips as I panted against him. "You think that was amazing? Baby, I've only just started."

With a deep thrust of his hips, he made me cry out again and again as he drove my body toward more delicious orgasms. He was relentless. Powerful. He knew how to use his cock and he wasn't afraid to show me.

Hours later, we fell into an exhausted sleep. Our bodies spent, the muscles between my legs swollen and deliciously tender from the most incredible night of sin.

Sometime before dawn, I slipped from the bed, careful not to wake him. As soon as my feet hit the floor they felt the empty condom wrappers we had discarded throughout our evening of debauchery. One. Two. Three. Four.

Yep. Four condoms and numerous, mind-blowing orgasms. Even now my body clenched and pulsed at the memory.

But this was where our story ended. It was time to hit the road.

I slipped into the bathroom and turned on the light. After peeing, I splashed water on my face and then stared at my reflection in the mirror. I had gotten what I had come here for. I had successfully fucked Charlie out of my mind, and there was no point hanging around to complicate things.

Again, my body pulsed and throbbed with the memory of that ten-inch cock and what it had done to me.

I dressed quickly, trying to be as quiet as possible so I didn't waken my one-night stand.

Before I turned off the light, I stared at the sexy bulk sprawled out across the bed. He was on his stomach, his muscular back and perfect ass on display, and I paused to take him in one last time.

"Good night, handsome," I whispered into the shadowy room.

Then, turning off the light, I slipped out the door and into the early morning.

CONNECT WITH ME ONLINE

Check these links for more books from Author Penny Dee.

READER GROUP

For more mayhem follow:
Kings of Mayhem MC Facebook page.
http://www.facebook.com/TheKingsofMayhemMC/

GOODREADS

Add my books to your TBR list on my Goodreads profile.
https://www.goodreads.com/author/show/8526535.Penny_Dee

AMAZON

Click to buy my books from my Amazon profile.
https://www.amazon.com/Penny-Dee/e/
B00O2OKT5G/ref=dp_byline_cont_ebooks_1

WEBSITE

http://www.pennydeebooks.com/

Penny Dee

INSTAGRAM
@authorpennydee

EMAIL
authorpennydee@hotmail.com

FACEBOOK
http://www.facebook.com/pennydeebooks/

ABOUT THE AUTHOR

Penny Dee writes contemporary romance about rockstars, bikers, hockey players and everyone in-between. She believes true love never runs smoothly, and her characters realize this too, with a boatload of drama and a whole lot of steam.

She found her happily ever after in Australia where she lives with her husband, daughter and a dog named Bindi.

Printed in Great Britain
by Amazon

82825933R00129